MW00764625

The Magic Ice Cream

and

Other Stories

by

ENID BLYTON

Illustrated by
Lesley Smith

AWARD PUBLICATIONS LIMITED

For further information on Enid Blyton please visit *www.blyton.com*

ISBN 978-1-84135-422-4

First published by Award Publications Limited 2000
This edition first published 2005

Published by Award Publications Limited,
The Old Riding School, The Welbeck Estate,
Worksop, Nottinghamshire, S80 3LR

12 5

Printed in the United Kingdom

CONTENTS

The
Magic Ice Cream

Once, when Tick and Tock, the two brownies, were sitting in their garden enjoying two strawberry ice creams they had just bought, a witch came by. As she passed, the tip of her cloak blew up and touched Tock's ice cream.

He grew red with excitement. "Did you see that?" he said to Tick. "That's made my ice cream a wishing ice! Whatever I wish will come true! Oh my, oh my, what luck!"

"I wish for six ice creams!" said Tick, at once. Immediately six lovely ice creams appeared on the table. Tock stared at them in surprise and anger.

"Tick! You're not to use my wishes. This is my magic ice, not yours. I wish all those six ices away!"

At once the ices disappeared, before Tick had even eaten a mouthful of them. He was very angry.

"Mean thing!" he shouted. "I'd let you share my wishes if I had any! I wish for my ices to come back!"

At once they all appeared again and Tick started eating one.

"And I wish them all away!" yelled Tock, in a temper. Off they went, in a twink.

"I wish you had a strawberry ice down your neck!" Tick shouted angrily.

"Ooh! Ah! Ooh!" Tock squealed as a large strawberry ice suddenly squeezed itself down his neck. "You horrid thing, Tick! I wish you had some hot cocoa down your back!"

Then it was Tick's turn to squeal as hot cocoa trickled down his back and burned him.

"Stop it, Tock, stop it burning me!" he begged. Tock laughed loudly when he saw Tick wriggling about, and that made Tick very angry.

"I wish you had no shoes on and had to

walk on prickly hedgehogs!" he cried.
Oh dear – poor Tock! At once his shoes
flew off and he found himself walking
on a hundred prickly hedgehogs, which
squealed and ran about. Tock at once
wished them away again, but his feet
were very much pricked and scratched.

7

He glared at Tick, who began to look frightened, afraid of what Tock would wish for him.

"Listen, Tock, listen," he said, quickly. "This is silly of us. We are wasting good wishes. Let us wish for good things, things we really want, instead of teasing each other like this."

"I've a good mind to wish you at the bottom of the sea!" grumbled Tock, sitting down and putting on his shoes.

"Oh no, Tock, *dear* Tock, don't do such a dreadful thing as that!" begged Tick. "Remember, we are brothers and we live together and are fond of one another."

"Well, don't you keep wishing then, because this is my magic ice, and not yours," Tock said sulkily. "I shall wish the wishes for both of us. You're not to wish at all. Do you hear?"

"Very well, Tock," said Tick. "Tell me when I may choose a wish, please."

"I am going to wish a wish for myself first," said Tock. He thought for a minute. "I wish for a very fine suit of gold," he said. At once his tunic, stockings, shoes and hat changed into gleaming gold, and Tick cried out at the sight of him.

"You look just like a prince, Tock!" he cried. "Wish for a suit like that for me."

"I wish Tick a very fine suit of silver," said Tock, who didn't wish Tick to be quite so fine as himself. Tick was disappointed and sulked.

"And now I wish for a fine horse!" said Tock. At once a beautiful black horse cantered into the garden. Tock was rather frightened.

"Ooh!" said Tick, surprised. "Wish me one like that, Tock!"

But Tock wasn't going to let Tick be as grand as he was. Oh no! "I wish a fine donkey for Tick!" he cried. A little grey donkey trotted up to Tick, but he cried out in rage.

"Tock! You mean thing! You've only wished me a suit of silver, instead of gold, and now you've got me a donkey instead of a horse. I wish them all away!"

Off went the horse and the donkey and away went the suits of gold and silver! Tock stared at Tick in a great rage. Then he rushed at him and hit him on the nose.

Tick cried out with pain and rushed at Tock. He knocked him over and Tock banged his head against the leg of a garden chair. He sat up and began to cry. Tick cried too, for his nose began to bleed.

"My n-n-n-nose is b-b-bleeding!" he sobbed.

"And I've a fearful b-b-b-bump!" wept Tock.

"Let's go indoors and bathe your nose and my bump, Tick."

So in they went, sorry for themselves and beginning to feel sorry for each other. Tock sponged Tick's nose and Tick sponged Tock's bruise.

"Let's not quarrel, Tick," said Tock.

"We've wasted all those wishes, you know. They've gone."

"I won't quarrel any more," wept Tick. "Let's be kind and generous, Tock, and not spoil things for one another. As soon as we get outside, you wish for something nice for yourself, and I promise I won't spoil it."

"No – I'll wish for something lovely for you!" said Tock, generously.

They went outside and sat down to think what lovely things to wish for – and then Tock saw a dreadful thing. While they had been indoors, the sun had melted the magic ice cream, and the next-door cat was licking it up! Imagine it! Licking up an enchanted ice cream! Tock drove the cat away – but it was too late. There was no ice cream left.

So it wasn't any good wishing. The ice cream was gone and the magic with it. It was very sad, very upsetting. Tock cried big tears and so did Tick.

"All we've g-g-got is a hurt n-n-nose and a b-b-bumped head!" sobbed Tock.

"Never mind, Tock," said Tick, putting

his arms round the other brownie. "We'll know better next time."

"There won't be a n-n-next time!" wept poor Tock. "We shall never have such a ch-ch-chance again!"

And you know, I'm very much afraid they never will!

The Dirty
Little Boy

There was once a boy called Tom, who seemed always to be dirty. It really didn't matter at all what he was doing – maybe only reading quietly in a chair – but when he got up he was sure to have dirty hands, knees and face, and probably a hole in his shirt.

"I can't help it, Mum!" he would say. "I don't mean to – the dirt just comes!"

Now there came a day when the schoolchildren had been promised a great treat. There was a wonderful circus in the town, and the headmaster had said that he would take the whole school that afternoon.

"You will be here punctually at two o'clock," he said to the listening boys and girls. "And you will come with clean hands, faces and knees, and your best clothes on. There will be a great many people at the circus, and I want them to look at you and say: 'What clean, well-behaved children!' And not: 'What a set of ragamuffins!' Anyone who arrives dirty will be left behind."

The children ran home joyfully. No school that afternoon – but a circus instead! What a treat!

Tom ran home too and told his mother.

"My goodness," she said, "you will really have to be clean for once, Tom! Hurry up with your lunch. I think I'll give you a good scrub – and then you can put on your best clothes."

So Tom hurried up, and very soon he was standing in the bathroom and his mother was scrubbing his knees and hands and washing his face and ears.

"Now give your teeth a clean, Tom," she said. "You might as well do that too."

At twenty minutes to two you should have seen Tom! He shone with soap and water! His teeth gleamed. His collar was as white as snow. His clothes were clean and quite perfect – he really was a fine sight to look at, for even his hair, which would usually stick straight up, was lying smooth and shining, flat on his round head.

"Well, you look nicer than I have ever seen you look before," said his mother, giving him a kiss. "Now off you go – and if you get to school as clean as that, you'll do!"

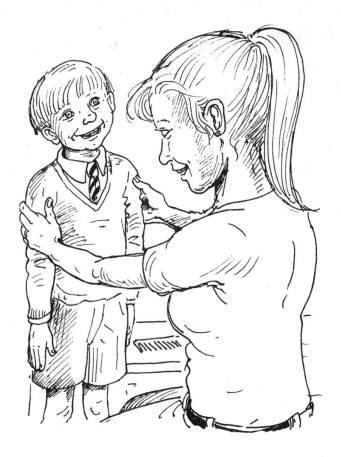

"Mum, I promise you I'll do my best," Tom said earnestly. "I like being clean, really I do. I don't know how it is I seem to get dirty. I will really be a good boy and go straight to school this very minute."

Off he went, walking carefully in the very middle of the pavement and going round every puddle instead of through it as he usually did. And he was very nearly at school when he heard something that puzzled him.

There was a shed nearby that led into a big dairy – and from this shed, or rather from underneath the shed, came a pitiful whining. Tom couldn't make it out. He looked into the shed – no one was there at all, certainly no dog. Then the whining came again, and Tom looked down at the floor for it seemed that the noise came from there.

And then he saw that a drainpipe came out of the shed from beneath the floor. It ran from the dairy, under the floor of the shed, and out into the road. The dog must be in there! It had got in – and it couldn't get out!

"Whatever shall I do?" wondered Tom. "All right, all right, good dog! I'm here! I've heard you! Good dog! don't be frightened!"

Tom kneeled down on the pavement

and looked down the pipe. Then he remembered that he had a torch in his pocket, so he took it out and flashed it down the hole. He saw the gleam of the dog's eyes quite clearly. The dog whined when it saw the light.

"I believe it's just frightened," thought Tom. "It doesn't dare to go backwards or forwards. I'll tell Mr Tucker, the milkman. Perhaps he can help me."

He ran through the shed into the dairy and called Mr Tucker, who was there. Together they went back and looked down the pipe.

"Have you got a bone or something?" asked Tom. "If you have, we might put it on a bit of string and throw it down the pipe. Then the dog would smell it and perhaps come up after it!"

"That's a good idea!" said the milkman. He went into his house next door to the dairy and fetched a big bone. Tom tied it on to a piece of string and then threw the bone down the pipe. The dog smelled it and whined eagerly, for it was hungry. It began to struggle upwards, and Tom laughed in delight.

"My trick's working!" he said. "He's coming all right! Good dog, good dog!"

The dog got almost to the pipe opening and then seemed to get stuck again. Tom had pulled the bone away as the dog got nearer to it, for he wanted the animal to come right up to the opening. Now he untied the string and left the bone by the pipe opening.

"I believe I could put my hand in and reach him now," said Tom. So he lay down on the pavement, put in his arm and felt about for the dog's collar. He took hold of it and tugged. The dog came out with a rush – and there he was on the pavement beside Tom, eagerly gnawing the bone!

"Good!" said the milkman, looking down at him. "What a nice little dog! I wonder who it belongs to. I'll look at his collar and see."

Just then the church clock struck two! Tom jumped – and looked down at his clothes. "Two o'clock!" he said. "I'm supposed to be at school – we're going to the circus, and look at the mess I'm in!"

"You certainly do look dirty," said Mr Tucker. "Your clothes are all dusty – and your hair is in a dreadful mess too. Come indoors and get yourself clean."

"Oh, I can't do that," said Tom. "I shall be too late. I must go as I am."

"All right," said the milkman. "I'll take the dog back to his owner. Hurry, now, or you'll be too late for the circus."

Tom rushed off, thinking that perhaps he might have time to wash at school – but as he slipped in, he saw his class marching into the big hall. His teacher caught sight of him and beckoned him to take his place at once.

Poor Tom! He took his place in the line, hot, dirty and untidy. And, most unfortunately, his class were right at the front, just by the platform on which the headmaster stood. Tom ran his hand

over his hair to make it straight, and rubbed his face with his handkerchief. He did hope the headmaster would not look at him.

"Now, you are all here, I hope," said the master pleasantly. "And how clean and tidy you look – really I feel proud of you! Hair well-brushed – clothes all tidy – faces clean… but wait a moment! WHO is this boy in front?"

Of course, it was poor Tom! There he stood, blushing red.

"Come out!" said the headmaster, in an awful voice. Tom stood out.

"What is this I see?" said the master, looking Tom up and down. "Dirty hands

– black knees – and unwashed face – scruffy clothes – hair anyhow! How DARE you come to school like this after what I have said?"

"Sir, I f-f-found a dog in a pipe," began Tom, but the headmaster frowned so much that he stopped, afraid to go on.

"I have heard what a dirty little boy you always are," said the headmaster, sternly. "Well, this time you shall be punished. You will stay here by yourself and write out 'I must keep clean' one hundred times in your best writing. I will NOT take a ragamuffin like you to the circus."

Tom went to his classroom, his eyes

full of tears. He was very unhappy indeed – and a good many tears dropped on to his book when he heard the sound of the other children walking down the street to the circus. It was to begin at three o'clock. How he wished he could be there!

"But I'm not sorry I got that dog out," he thought. "I just had to do that. I couldn't leave it. I never thought about getting dirty."

Now the milkman had looked at the dog's collar, and to his surprise he saw printed on it: *Toby, Miller's Circus.*

"Why, it's a circus dog!" he said, in astonishment. "I'd better take him back at once. He may be wanted this afternoon for all I know. Perhaps he is a performing dog."

So he put the dog on a lead and took him to the gate that led into the circus field. He told the man there about the dog, and he was at once taken to a caravan behind the tents.

"Hey, Joe!" called the gate man. "Here's someone with your dog! Just in time too!"

A man looked out of the caravan. He had the white face of a clown, and was dressed in clown's clothes. When he saw the dog he gave a whoop of delight, and ran down the caravan steps at once.

"Why, Toby, Toby boy!" he said. "Where have you been? I was getting so worried about you." Then he turned to the milkman. "That's the cleverest dog in the circus!" he said. "He always performs with me – and the things he does! He is a clown dog, I always say. I didn't know what I was going to do without him, I can tell you! I am much obliged to you for bringing him. Would you like free tickets for the circus?"

"Well," said the milkman, "you oughtn't really to thank me. I didn't get him for you. He was down a drainpipe under my shed, and a small boy found him there, and got him out by means of a bone on a string. Your dog had got stuck there through fright or something. He might have been there for days if young Tom Allen hadn't found him."

"Well, I'll have to go and thank him, then," said the clown. "I expect he'll be with all the school children at the circus this afternoon, won't he? There they are, look, in the seats over there – just sitting down in them."

The milkman looked. "I can't see young Tom," he said. "But I expect he'll be there. Look, that's the headmaster. If you go and ask him, he'll tell you which boy is Tom Allen. Now I must go. Goodbye – and good luck to the show!"

Off went Mr Tucker. The clown

finished dressing himself, and then dressed Toby the dog in a clown's costume too. At once the little dog began to prance about and behave very comically. He knew quite well that the circus was about to begin!

"Come on, Toby, we'll go and find your rescuer now," said the clown. So with Toby jumping beside him he walked into the ring and up to the headmaster, who was sitting in the front row.

"Good afternoon, sir," said the clown. "Would you mind telling me which of your boys is Tom Allen? He rescued my dog from a drainpipe this afternoon, so I've been told – and I've got him back just in time for the show! I'd like to thank the boy who got him out of the pipe."

"Tom Allen!" said the master. "Why, we left him behind – he came to school so dirty and untidy that I couldn't bring him."

"I suppose he got like that getting Toby out of the pipe," said the clown. "Well – it's rather hard that because he helped someone belonging to the circus, he's

not allowed to come and see it!"

"I'd no idea that was what he had been doing," said the headmaster. "Is that so, really? Well – we must see what can be done. Perhaps he could come tomorrow."

"Look here, sir, there are ten minutes still before we begin," said the clown. "Will you let me go and get the boy? It won't take me more than five minutes on my bike. I don't like to think of him there all alone – when he did such a good turn for my dog!"

"Very well," said the headmaster. "I don't like to think of it either – poor Tom! Go to the school, and tell him I know all about it and that he can come back with you!"

Off went Joe the clown. He got his bike and was soon pedalling away up the street to the school. He was there in three minutes and ran in at the door.

Tom was still writing out *I must keep clean* when he heard the sound of footsteps going in and out of the classrooms. He wondered who it was – and he was even more surprised when he saw a circus clown coming in at the door! He sat and stared as if he couldn't believe his eyes.

"Hello," said the clown. "Are you Tom Allen? Well, young fellow-me-lad, you're to come along with me! It was my dog you got out of the pipe – and when I went to ask the headmaster which of his boys you were he told me he'd left you here! And when I told him about my dog he sent me to find you and bring you to the circus after all. So get your cap and hurry.

Do you want to wash first? You look a bit dirty."

Tom gave a loud shout of joy and rushed to the cloakroom to wash himself. It didn't take him long. The clown brushed his clothes for him, and then Tom stood on the bicycle step and the clown rode swiftly back to the circus taking the small boy with him.

It had just begun. All the performers were walking into the ring, and a man was beating an enormous drum. The

schoolchildren were clapping madly.

"I must leave you now," said the clown. "Go to the headmaster and tell him I've fetched you. Hope you enjoy the show! Come round to my caravan afterwards and see me. Ask for Joey."

He ran off, and soon was capering about the ring with the other clowns, his dog Toby jumping beside him, falling over whenever his master fell, and behaving just like a little clown-dog!

Tom made his way through the children and came up to his headmaster. He stood behind his seat, and at last the Head turned and saw him.

"Hello, it's you, Tom," he said. "So the clown fetched you as he said. Well – it was all a mistake. For once in a way you really couldn't help being dirty, could you? Sit down here beside me and join us."

How they laughed at the clowns, and cheered the beautiful horses dancing in time to the music, and stared in wonder at the acrobats. It was the finest circus you could imagine – and how glad Tom

was that he was not left behind at school writing out *I must keep clean* a hundred times!

"Thank you for my seat, sir, and for sending Joey to get me," said Tom, at the end. "And, sir – I will try to look a bit cleaner in future! I won't let you down again!"

"I take your word for it!" said the Head, and patted him on the shoulder. "Now – I suppose you want to go and say goodbye to your friend the clown, don't you? Well, hurry off, and see you come clean to school tomorrow morning!"

Tom shot off, and found his way to the caravan where Joey sat eating an enormous tea of shrimps, new bread and iced cake. He was pleased to see Tom.

"Sit down," he said. "Have some tea? Go on – there's plenty. Toby and I are pleased to share anything with a boy like you! We won't forget things in a hurry – will we, Toby?"

"Wuff!" said Toby, and wagged his tail.

"You can come to the circus each day we are here," said the clown, generously. "Tell the man at the gate that you are Joey's friend – and he'll let you in. See!"

"Oh, thank you very much indeed," said Tom, delighted. "I say – I am lucky! I thought when I was left behind this afternoon that I wasn't going to go to the circus at all – and I've been after all – and I'll go every day as well!"

"Ah, you never know your luck," said Joey, wisely. "The best thing is to do what you can for others – and sure enough, others will do what they can for you! Isn't that right, Toby dog?"

And Toby wagged his tail hard and said "Wuff!" – so Joey must have been right!

Good
Gracious Me!

It all happened in such a hurry! Leslie was going along the path in the wood on his bicycle, thinking of what he would spend his pocket money on. He was wishing he could save up enough money to buy a bell to put on the handlebar of his bicycle.

"Sometimes I go almost as fast as a car, and I really ought to have a bell to warn people to get out of the way!" thought Leslie.

Just then somebody rushed by him, almost knocking him over. Leslie was cross. "Hi! Don't go rushing about like that!" he shouted. Then he stared in surprise.

The person who had nearly knocked him over was the longest-legged man he had ever seen! Leslie stared after him. He had long spidery legs, long arms, and a long neck on which sat a big head with pointed ears!

"He must be a gnome or a pixie or something!" said Leslie. And just as he was thinking that, he heard shouts behind him. "Stop him! Stop thief! Hi, can't you stop him?"

Then two or three very small men rushed all round Leslie. He thought they must be goblins. They looked very cross and impatient.

"Why didn't you stop him? Didn't you see Long-Legs rushing by? He's taken a bag of magic spells from us!"

"Oh," said Leslie, in surprise. "Well, I didn't know that. Anyway, he's gone. You'll never catch him, he's got such long legs!"

"Lend us your bicycle!" said one of the goblins, and caught hold of it. "Come on! Lend it to us! We can go fast on this."

"No," said Leslie, who felt sure he would never see his nice new bicycle again if he let the little men have it.

"Yes!" said the little men, and they all jumped on the bicycle at once, with Leslie in the middle of them, and then they made Leslie pedal very quickly. The bicycle simply shot through the trees!

"Let me slow down! We'll have an accident!" said Leslie. But he might as well have spoken to the moon. The little men shouted at him to pedal faster and faster. They held on to Leslie and to each other; it must have been a funny sight to see them tearing along at top speed through the wood!

"There he is! Go on, faster, faster!" yelled the little man who was right in front.

And faster they went, till Leslie could hardly breathe! Then *crash*! They bumped into a tree and all of them fell off. The front wheel of the bicycle looked a little bent. But the little men took no notice of that! No, up they all jumped again, nearly leaving poor Leslie behind this time, and off they went again, with Leslie clinging to the handlebars for all he was worth.

"I can see him! I can see Long-Legs!" yelled the front goblin. "He's going to the goblin market. That's where he's going. He means to sell our spells there. Hurry!"

They left the path in the wood and came out on a main road. Leslie knew he had never been there before. It was crowded with all kinds of fairy folk! How he stared.

"We shall knock people over. Look out!" he shouted. "I'm going too fast."

"Ring your bell, then, ring it, ring it!" yelled the little men.

"I haven't got one!" said Leslie. "I must slow down. I nearly knocked over that pixie."

"We'd better stop and buy a bell," said the little man at the front. "We don't want an accident."

So they stopped at a little shop and bought a most wonderful bell. It looked

like silver to Leslie, and how it shone.
They fixed it on to the handlebar.

Then on they tore again, this time
ringing for all they were worth. *Ting-a-
ling*! *Ting-a-ling*! *Ting-a-ling*!

People hopped out of the way at once.
The bicycle raced on as fast as an express
train. Leslie couldn't help enjoying it,
especially as he was the one to ring
the bell!

"There's Long-Legs again!" yelled the little men. "Faster, faster!"

Ting-a-ling! *Ting-a-ling*! On they went and, just as they reached the crowded market, they caught up with Long-Legs. In fact they ran right into him, and knocked him over! Everyone fell off the bicycle, and then the goblins swarmed over the groaning Long-Legs like ants.

They took away his bag of spells and tied his hands behind him, and began to march him away.

"Hi!" called Leslie. "Tell me the way home!"

The goblins stopped. They seemed to have forgotten about Leslie, "Oh, don't you know it?" they called. "Well, never mind, your bicycle does. Just hop on and it will take you back to the path in the wood." Leslie was rather doubtful about this. He hadn't noticed that his bicycle was very clever before.

"Well, what about your bell?" he called. "Don't you want it?"

"Oh no. You can have it in return for letting us borrow your bicycle," called back the goblins. "Goodbye."

"Goodbye," said Leslie, and looked at his new bell in delight. Goodness, what would his mother say?

He got on his bicycle and pushed off. To his surprise and delight it raced along by itself, and he didn't even need to pedal again until he reached the path that he knew, in the middle of the wood.

There was no one about, of course, but Leslie couldn't help ringing his bell. *Ting-a-ling*! *Ting-a-ling*! And all the rabbits scuttled out of the way at once.

He got home at last, feeling quite tired. When he told his mother how he got his new bell, she didn't believe him.

"All right – I'll take you to the market and you'll see all I saw!"

But isn't it a pity – he can't find the way again now. Still, perhaps he will some day.

The
Boastful Prince

Once upon a time there was a little prince called Janni, who was very boastful. He was rich and well dressed, and because people bowed low to him whenever they met him, and praised him, he thought he was very wonderful.

"I am the cleverest boy in the world," he told the footmen.

"You are, Your Highness!" they said and they bowed themselves down to the ground.

"I am the smartest boy in the kingdom," said Janni to the butler.

"You are, Your Highness," said the butler, and bowed himself halfway to the ground.

As you can see, Janni was vain and boastful. He thought the world of himself, and nobody stopped him. His mother, the queen, thought he was a marvellous boy too. His father, King Nicholas, was too busy ruling the country to bother much about Janni.

One day Janni thought he would dress up as a country boy and have an adventure. It would be fun to go about and pretend to be someone ordinary.

So he got a smock from the son of one of the gardeners, and a pair of boots. He put the smock on over his fine suit, and laced up the boots. He put on an old hat, took a stick, and off he went.

He walked and he walked. He went over the hill and down by the river, and at last he came to a shady wood. It was a hot day and Janni felt tired. He went into the wood and sat down. Soon he heard someone coming along whistling.

He looked to see who it was. He saw a boy about his own age, and a girl a little smaller. They were carrying a basket between them. There was washing in it, for their mother was a washer-woman and lived in the woods.

46

"Hello!" said the boy and girl to Prince Janni.

"Hello!" said Janni.

"Like a game?" asked the boy. "My name's Will. This is my sister Lucy."

"My name's Janni," said the prince.

"Can you play leapfrog?" asked Will.

"Of course!" said Janni. "I can play anything! I am good at everything."

"Hark at him!" said Lucy. "He knows how to blow his own trumpet, anyway!"

"What does that mean?" asked Janni.

"Don't you know?" Will said scornfully. "It means that you know how to boast. We call it blowing your own trumpet."

"You are not very polite," said Janni. "I have better manners than you."

"I suppose you think you have better everything!" said Lucy. "How old are you?"

"Ten," said Janni, "and I am bigger for my age than any other boy in the kingdom."

"Pooh!" said Will. "I'm only nine – and I'm taller than you already!"

Janni jumped up and the two stood back to back. Will was right.

"Will is much taller than you!" cried Lucy. "You are not so tall, nor so clever as you think, Janni."

Janni went red. It was the first time anyone had ever spoken to him like that. He didn't like it.

"I am clever!" he said. "My mother says I am the most wonderful boy in the world."

"Mothers often say that," said Will. "My mother thinks the same of me. But all the same I know I'm not all that wonderful."

"Heaps and heaps of people have told me I am the cleverest boy in the kingdom," said Janni, remembering how all the servants at the palace had agreed with him when he said things like this.

"You can't be very clever, else you wouldn't have been so stupid as to believe them," said Lucy, with a giggle.

Janni glared at her.

"Ask me anything you like and I'll tell you the answer," he said, in a very stiff sort of voice. He had lessons every day with the wisest men in the kingdom and he had learned a great deal. He knew all about why the sea has tides, why we have night and day, and even how it is that we have spring, summer, autumn and winter. So he felt quite safe.

Lucy began to giggle again. "You are a funny boy," she said. "A real little boaster!"

"No, I'm not," said Janni, his face redder than ever. "Quick! Ask me something and I'll tell you the answer!"

"All right," said Will. "Tell me how many peas there are in a pint!"

Janni stared at Will. "You don't know that yourself," he said.

"Oh yes, I do!" said Will at once. "Go on – tell me. You say you're so clever!"

"I should have to see a pint of peas and count them," said Janni.

"Well, we'll take you to our house and give you a pint of peas to count," said Lucy. "But you won't get the answer right, will he, Will?"

"Have you any questions to ask me, Lucy?" asked Janni, walking beside the two children through the wood.

"Oh yes, I can ask you heaps – but you won't know the answers," said Lucy. "You are just a little stupid – not nearly as clever as the children at our village school."

Poor Janni really didn't know what to say! He walked along, quite determined to show these two children how clever he really was.

"I'll ask you my question," said Lucy. "Can you tell me how many bees there are in our back garden?"

"You don't know that yourself," said Janni.

"Yes, I do! I do!" sang Lucy, dancing up and down, so that the washing-basket

tipped up and nearly threw out the clothes. "I always know how many bees there are in our back garden."

"I can tell you the answer if I see your back garden," said Janni.

"Well, here we are," said Lucy. And sure enough, there they were – at the gate of the little cosy cottage, with a dear little flowery garden all round it. Bees were humming busily, and rows of peas, beans, and lettuces ran down one side.

"We're home, Mother, we're home!" shouted Lucy. A nice, jolly-faced woman came to the door and took the basket. She smiled at Janni.

"Mother, Mother, Janni says he knows how many peas there are in a pint, and he's going to find out how many bees there are in our back garden!" cried Will.

"Now don't you tease him too much," said their mother, who knew her two rascals very well indeed. "There are some cakes cooling on the window-sill. You can have one each."

"Oooh!" cried Lucy, and ran to get the cakes.

Soon they were all munching them. Then Lucy went to pick some peas, taking with her a pint-measure to put them in. Janni wanted to count them!

"I'd better begin counting the bees in the back garden," said Janni, as Lucy and Will picked the peas. So he began.

But it was really very difficult! The bees wouldn't keep still and be counted! They flew here and there, and just as Janni had counted one it would fly out of the garden! It was most annoying. More

bees kept flying in, and the little boy got into a dreadful muddle.

He didn't like to say so. Wasn't he the smartest boy in the kingdom? Didn't he know more than anyone else? Wasn't he much, much cleverer than these two children? Then how did Lucy know how many bees there were in her back garden and he couldn't count them at all?

"Perhaps I'll be better at the peas," said Janni to himself. "Here's Lucy with the pint-measure full. Now I'll soon know how many peas there are in a pint!"

He sat down with the pint-measure and began to count. It was very difficult. The peas kept slipping out of his fingers. He kept forgetting the number he had got to, and had to begin again. Lucy and Will giggled all the time and wouldn't stop.

"Whatever is there that is so funny about this?" asked Janni at last, getting quite cross.

"Oh, you don't know how funny you looked going round the garden counting the big and little bees!" said Lucy,

54

beginning to laugh again. "You poked your finger at one and counted it – and no sooner had you counted it than it flew over the hedge! And then lots more flew in – and you ran after them trying to count them before they went off again! And now you are wasting your time counting those peas!"

"And he thinks he's clever! He thinks he's smart!" laughed Will.

"Well, how do you know the number of peas in a pint without counting?" asked Janni crossly. "You must be clever if you can tell me without counting all these."

"I don't need to count them – I know!" giggled Lucy.

"Well, tell me then," said Janni. "How many peas are there in a pint?"

"Only one 'p' in a pint!" laughed Lucy. "Don't you know how to spell pint, silly? P-I-N-T! How many p's? Only one! And you've tried to count all those real peas!"

"And how many b's in back garden?" asked Will. "Can't you spell that either? B-A-C-K-G-A-R-D-E-N! Only one 'b' of course. Baby! Baby!"

Janni stared at the two children. So that was what they had meant! How stupid of him not to have guessed there was a trick in it! Perhaps he wasn't so clever after all. He felt cross – and very small.

"If you knew who I really was you wouldn't play these tricks on me," he said crossly.

"Well, who are you?" asked Lucy.

"I am Prince Janni," said the little boy, longing to lift up his smock and show them his grand clothes underneath.

The children shrieked with laughter.

They rolled on the grass and laughed till they cried.

"What will he say next?" they shouted.

"What is funny about that?" asked Janni, astonished.

"Well, who would want to be that

dreadful, vain, boastful little prince?" said Will, sitting up. "You can't know much about him, or you wouldn't want to pretend to be him. We all laugh at him and his silly, boastful ways. He's a perfect little stupid!"

Janni's eyes filled with tears. So that was what people thought of him! He was glad now that he hadn't lifted up his smock to show Lucy and Will his princely clothes below.

"Will! Lucy! Lunch-time!" called the children's mother. "Tell the little boy to go home!"

"Goodbye!" said the children. "Goodbye, Janni! You've got the same name as our prince – but don't get like him, whatever you do! Come and play another day."

Janni went back to the palace. He was ashamed of himself. He wanted to be nicer. He made up his mind not to boast any more.

His father, King Nicholas, came in, and Janni bowed to him, for he was the king. A smile crept over his face.

"Your Majesty, my father," he said, "can you tell me how many peas there are in a pint, and how many bees there are in our back garden?"

Will you believe it, the king didn't know! Ask your father and see if he knows. If he does, he's a cleverer man than King Nicholas!

Miggle and
Mr Stamp-About

There was once a funny little fellow called Miggle. He was a kindly creature, always ready with a joke and a smile, but he really was very stupid.

Everyone teased him. Everyone said he had no brains at all which was perfectly true. They just treated Miggle as a Great Big Joke.

And that made Miggle rather sad. He didn't want to be just a joke. He didn't want always to be laughed at. He badly wanted to feel grown-up and important, just sometimes. But nobody would let him.

One day Mr Stamp-About came to live in Miggle's village. He was a very bad-tempered fellow. He roared and shouted at everyone, he stamped about and made such a noise that the peaceful villagers were dreadfully scared.

"I wish he'd go away," said Jinky.

"I wish he'd never come," said Feefo.

"Let's tell him we don't want him in our village," said Tiptoe.

So they told him. But Mr Stamp-About went purple in the face and stamped so hard that he made a thick dust that choked everyone and made them cough.

"What! You dare to tell me what to do!" yelled Mr Stamp-About, his hair

standing straight on end. "Just wait till I catch one of you, that's all! I'll slap him till he's nothing but a trembling jelly!"

Now everyone knew quite well that Mr Stamp-About would certainly keep his word, so they all fled away at once. Nobody wanted to meet Stamp-About any more. Everyone went another way when they saw him.

And, as you can guess, poor little Miggle was more afraid than anyone. He just shivered in his shoes when he even heard Stamp-About's voice in the distance. For one thing, Miggle had once laughed loudly at Stamp-About when the wind had blown his hat off, and Stamp-About had never forgiven him for that.

"I know he would pull every hair out of my head, and swing me round by my nose or ears, and do something dreadful to me if he caught me," thought poor Miggle. So he didn't go near Stamp-About if he could possibly help it.

He was very glad when Feefo asked him to go over the hill to the next village to fetch him a barrel of apples.

"You may be a silly fellow, Miggle, but you're strong," said Feefo. "So go over to my aunt's and ask her to give you a barrel of red apples for me. Carry it back to me and I'll give you a gold penny."

"Right!" said Miggle, and set off. He got the barrel of apples, set it on his shoulder, and climbed to the top of the hill over which he had to go to get back to his own village.

And, oh dear me, goodness gracious, who should be coming up the hill-path but Mr Stamp-About himself! Miggle

knew he hadn't time to turn and go back down the hill, and he simply couldn't face Stamp-About. He didn't know what to do.

Then he had an idea. Stamp-About hadn't yet seen him. Miggle would empty out the apples and get inside the barrel. He could hide there quite well. Maybe Stamp-About would go right past him and not notice the barrel at all.

So in a great hurry Miggle emptied out the apples and got inside the barrel. It stood there on the hilltop, quite still.

But the apples rolled and bumped merrily down the hill! You should have seen them. They shot down the path and bumped into Stamp-About. He was most surprised. He thought someone was throwing them at him, and he was very angry. He began to shout.

"How dare you throw apples at me! How dare you! Wait till I get you! Oh, you'll be sorry for yourself then, you certainly will!"

Now Miggle heard all this and he began to shake like a jelly. He shook so

hard that he jerked the barrel over on to its side. And, of course, the barrel began to roll down the hill! Down it went and down, going faster and faster as it went. It leaped over stones and made a tremendous noise – *clitter, clatter, bang, crash, bump, clatter*!

Miggle was being turned over and over inside as the barrel shot down the hill. He felt terribly giddy and very frightened, but he just couldn't do anything about it.

Stamp-About heard the noise and looked to see what it was. When he saw the big barrel coming jumping down the hill-path, he was really scared. He turned to run.

Down the path he went, with the barrel after him, going *clitter, clatter, bang, crash, bump, clatter!*

"It's chasing me, it's chasing me!"

cried Stamp-About, in a dreadful fright. "Stop it, somebody, stop it!"

The little folk of the village had come out to watch. They laughed till their sides ached when they saw what was happening. As for stopping the barrel, well, no one was going to do that! No – let it catch Stamp-About if it could!

Stamp-About got to the bottom of the hill, panting and shouting. The barrel got there too, rolling very fast indeed. It bumped over a tree-root, sprang high into the air, and landed right on top of Stamp-About! He went down, *bump*, just like a skittle.

"It's caught me, it's caught me!" he yelled. "Oh, save me, save me!"

But nobody saved him. The barrel rolled a little way off, and then stayed still.

Stamp-About got up. He was covered with bruises. He looked in fright at the barrel.

"Run, Stamp-About, before it chases you again!" cried the little folk. And Stamp-About ran. How he ran! He ran

and he ran – and he never came back. He was gone for ever.

After a while, poor bruised, giddy Miggle stuck his head up out of the barrel. Everyone stared at him in great astonishment. Miggle looked at Feefo. He was very much afraid that Feefo would scold him for losing all his apples.

But nobody scolded him at all. To Miggle's enormous surprise they all crowded round him and patted him wherever they could reach him.

"Miggle! You clever fellow! So it was you who thought of that marvellous idea," they cried. "Why, Miggle, you are Simply Wonderful."

"No, I'm not," said Miggle. "You see – I was afraid – and I…"

But nobody would let him explain. They all thought he had done a really marvellous thing, and was a great hero. So Miggle began to smile and feel very happy indeed.

And now at last Miggle is no longer treated as a joke. He is Somebody! People listen to him, and tell him he is a grand fellow. Well, well – it may have been an accident that he chased Stamp-About away, but it did old Miggle a lot of good, didn't it!

The Monkey Up
the Tree

"Oh, gosh – what's that animal sitting on the fence – look!" James cried suddenly as he went home from school one autumn afternoon.

All the children stopped and stared. The animal was small and brown and furry, and it had a long tail. It stared back at the children.

"It's a monkey!" said Hilary. "It is, really! Wherever has it come from? There's no circus near here."

"It's a dear little thing," said Jenny. "It looks cold – see how it shivers. I think we ought to tell the police or somebody. It might die if it has to be out-of-doors on a cold night."

"Let's see if it's tame," said James. "If it is, perhaps it would let us catch it and cuddle it up in one of our coats."

So they went cautiously up to the fence but as soon as it saw them coming near, the monkey was off and away! It scampered along the top of the fence, and then went into Mr Ritchie's orchard.

"It's up an apple-tree!" said Hilary. "Do monkeys like apples?"

Nobody knew. They stood and watched the little creature. As they stood there, looking over the wall of the orchard, a man came out of the nearby house and shouted at them.

"Now then, you kids! Clear off! I know what you're after, standing there, staring over my wall. You want my apples!"

"We don't!" called back James at once. "We're looking at a monkey up a tree."

"Monkey up a tree! What will you say next?" shouted Mr Ritchie. "You don't expect me to believe that, do you?"

"Well, it's true!" called Hilary.

But Mr Ritchie wasn't going to believe a tale like that! He shook his walking-stick at them. "You clear off home!"

"We don't want your apples!" shouted back George, joining in crossly. "We're not thieves."

"Oh yes, you are – children are all alike, stealing whenever they can," shouted Mr Ritchie. "Who took my plums? Who took my cherries? You did! But you're not going to take my apples."

"Isn't he horrid?" said James. "It's only those two boys, Andrew and Paul, who climb over and take his apples. They really are bad boys. What are we going to do about that monkey?"

"We'll call at the police station," said

Hilary. She looked at the rosy-red apples growing thickly on the trees over the wall. They were sweet and ripe.

"I wish I had one of those apples!" she said. "You know, James, the man who lived here before Mr Ritchie used to let four of the best children from school come and fill baskets each week to take for their classes to eat. Oooh – they were delicious!"

"Mr Ritchie's too mean – and he doesn't like children," said Jenny. Then she gave a little scream.

Two boys had crept quietly up behind her and had tweaked her long plaits. "Andrew! Paul! You horrid things!" cried Jenny. "Leave my plaits alone!"

The two boys grinned. "What are you all doing here? We heard Mr Ritchie shouting at you. Were you stealing his apples? Oh, naughty, naughty!"

"Of course we weren't!" said Hilary, indignantly. "We were looking at that monkey – see, up in the tree over there."

The two boys looked. They were astonished to see a monkey there. Andrew immediately picked up a stone, but Jenny knocked it out of his hand.

"No. NO, you're not to throw stones at him!" she said angrily. "You'll hurt him. He's frightened enough already."

Then Paul picked up a stone and flung it at the monkey. It hit the bough near him and made him jump. He made a little chattering noise.

"Nearly got him!" said Paul. "You have a go, Andrew – you're a better shot than I am."

The other children tried to stop this

stone-throwing, but the two boys were stronger than they were. Stones flew through the air, and one hit the little monkey on his front paw. He gave a yelp and leaped into another tree, where he sat nursing his hurt paw just like a child.

"You beast!" said Jenny, and slapped Paul hard. He dodged and threw another stone.

And then things began to happen! The monkey, hit again, this time on his tail, began to chatter angrily. He pulled off an apple hanging near his head and took aim. He flung it with all his might at Paul and hit him full on the head – *thud*!

Paul was startled. He didn't know what had hit him – but the other children did. They roared with laughter.

Then the monkey began to throw apples in earnest! He picked them as fast as he could and flung them at all the children, not knowing which were his friends and which his enemies!

They dodged as the apples came flying fast, dropping with a thud and a bounce on to the road. Soon there were dozens lying around!

Half laughing, half frightened, Hilary and the others dodged here and there. The two big boys were hit three times each and didn't like it! Nobody else was hit – it really almost seemed as if the

monkey was trying to hit Paul and Andrew now!

The children grew scared after a little while, when about a hundred apples lay all over the place. "I'd better slip home and get my barrow," said George, who lived just round the corner. "Then we can pick them up and put them in it, and wheel them to Mr Ritchie."

So he fetched his barrow and everyone except Paul and Andrew picked up apples and filled the little barrow. The other two filled their pockets instead!

Then suddenly, round the corner came a big policeman. When he saw what the children were doing he hurried up at once, frowning. Andrew and Paul tried to run away, but he caught hold of them.

"Now, what's all this?" he said. "Stealing apples! Taking them away in a barrow! I never heard anything like it! What are your names?"

"*We're* not stealing them," said Hilary, indignantly. "There's a monkey up a tree over there – and when Paul and Andrew threw stones at him, he threw apples back."

"But these two boys have got apples in their pockets," said the policeman,

sternly. "That won't do! Do you want me to go to your fathers?"

"No – no, please don't," said both boys, frightened at once. They took out the apples from their pockets and threw them quickly into the barrow. The policeman still had hold of them.

"Did I hear you say something about a monkey?" he asked Hilary. "Where is it? A monkey has been reported missing this afternoon by Mr Ritchie's sister."

"It's up there," said George, pointing, and the policeman suddenly saw it still nursing its paw.

Then the door of the house flew open and out rushed Mr Ritchie again, in a rage. "What's all this, Constable?" he shouted. "Have you caught some children taking my apples? I'll…"

He caught sight of the barrow full of apples and stopped in amazement. "Why – look at all those apples! How dare they steal such a lot? I'll… I'll…"

"We didn't steal them!" said Jenny, in tears. "The monkey threw them at us. Those boys threw stones at him and he threw apples back – and we've just fetched a barrow and picked them all up to bring back to you."

"Monkey? A monkey that throws apples? I don't believe a word of it!" said Mr Ritchie, shaking his walking-stick again. And then, at that very moment, frightened by the farmer's shouting, the monkey threw another apple! It hit the

farmer on the head and knocked off his hat. He was most astonished.

"There you are – that was the monkey again!" said Hilary. "Good shot, monkey!"

"Excuse me, Mr Ritchie, sir," said the policeman, politely. "I think that's your sister's monkey. She telephoned to say it had escaped from her house two streets away. Maybe as it has often been to your house with your sister, sir, it came here, knowing the way. And these two boys teased it, and threw stones at it – so it threw apples back."

"Hm! Er – well really – what an extraordinary thing," said Mr Richie, looking quite red in the face. "My sister's monkey? Yes, now I can see it is. Mickey, Mickey, come here, you rascal!" And the monkey scampered down the tree at once, leaped up to the fence and into Mr Ritchie's arms, where he cuddled down, chattering happily.

"Shall I wheel these apples into your garden for you, Mr Ritchie?" asked James, politely. "Mickey picked and threw every one of them!"

"Er – no – no, thank you. I'd like you to keep them for yourselves," said Mr Ritchie. "I'm sorry I thought you'd picked them." Then he swung round on Paul and Andrew and frowned so fiercely at them that they cowered away.

"But you're not to have any!" he said. "No, not one. Shame on you for stoning this little creature, shame on you, I say. Be off with you!"

Paul and Andrew fled away at top speed. The others helped themselves to an apple each, very pleased.

"Thank you, sir," said James. "We shall love to have these apples. We'll wheel them to school tomorrow and let everyone help themselves. Thanks very much!" And off they went, munching happily.

"What an exciting afternoon!" said Jenny. "I never thought a monkey would pick apples for us, did you?"

"You simply never know what's going to happen!" said George. And he's certainly right!

Fussy
Philip

Once upon a time there was a boy who made a fuss about everything. You really would have laughed if you had lived in his home, to see the way he made a fuss about even the very smallest things.

The fussing began each morning when he got up. He always wanted to wear something different from what his mother said he should wear.

"Oh dear! Must I wear that red jersey today?" he would say. "I do hate it. It's tight at my neck."

"But you loved wearing it yesterday!" his mother would say in surprise. "Well, wear the blue one."

"Oh, Mum, that's too thick," Philip would say. And then he would fuss about his shoes.

"I don't want to wear my sandals. The boys laugh at them. And my lace ones have a nail inside that sticks into my foot. Oh dear, what shall I wear?"

At mealtimes the fussing was terrible. If there were eggs, Philip would pout and say, "I don't like eggs. I want fish."

And if there was fish he would poke at it with his fork and fuss about bones. "I am sure there are bones in my fish cake, I'm sure there are. I shall get one in my throat and it will choke me."

"Don't be silly, Philip," his mother would say patiently. "There aren't bones in fish cakes."

"Well, I had a bone in one last week," Philip would grumble. "Can't I have an egg?"

Everyone at school called him Fussy Philip. He fussed about his books. He fussed about his pencils. He fussed because someone else hung their coat on his peg by mistake.

One day he fussed so much that his teacher got really angry with him. She had told the class to rule some straight lines in their geography books, so Philip had opened his desk to get out his book.

"Oh my, where's it gone?" he fussed. "I know I put it here with my history book. Miss Brown, did I give my book to you yesterday? I can't find it."

"Don't make such a fuss," said Miss Brown. "I expect it's somewhere in your desk. Look carefully and don't chatter so much."

Well, of course, the book was there, next to the history books after all. But then Philip couldn't find his ruler. He began to fuss all over again.

"Who's taken my ruler? Has anyone

borrowed my ruler? Oh bother, bother,
now my ruler's gone! Miss Brown, I've
got my geography book but I haven't got
my ruler."

"Be quiet, Philip," said Miss Brown,
who was getting very tired of him.
"Borrow John's. He's finished ruling his
lines."

"But, Miss Brown, what can have
happened to my ruler?" fussed Philip.
"Honestly, it was here this morning. I

don't want to borrow John's. It's a bit broken at the edge and it doesn't make nice lines. I want my own ruler."

"Philip, if you don't borrow someone else's and get on, the lesson will be over before you've even begun it!" said Miss Brown. "Look – isn't that your ruler on the top of your desk?"

"Oh, good gracious me, yes, it is!" Philip said. "Of course, I remember now. I got it out first and put it there. And all this time I've been hunting in my desk. How funny!"

"It's not a bit funny," said Miss Brown crossly. "It's just silly. Do stop fussing and get on."

John, who sat next to Philip, took up his pen and shook it. It was a fine new fountain pen, just filled with ink. A drop flew from the nib and landed on Philip's jersey sleeve. How he fussed again!

"Miss Brown! Oh, Miss Brown, do look what John has done! He's shaken a blob of ink on to my jersey sleeve. Oh, Miss Brown, my mother will be cross, won't she?"

"PHILIP! Be quiet," said Miss Brown, in quite a fierce tone. "Your jersey is dark blue and the ink is dark blue and the blob won't show at all when it's dry. Press a bit of blotting-paper on it."

"Miss Brown, now my blotting-paper is gone!" said Philip, rummaging through his desk in a hurry. "Oh, goodness, who's borrowed that now? It was such a nice new piece. My mother gave it to me yesterday. Miss Brown, may I have a new piece out of the cupboard, please?"

"Philip, I'm tired of you," said Miss Brown suddenly. "I never met such a

fusser in all my life. If you say one word more about anything in this class, you can just go and put on your coat and cap and go home. You hold up the whole class with your silly fussing."

Well, Philip got rather a shock when Miss Brown said that. He didn't say one word more but got on with his work. But the fussing began all over again when playtime came after the lesson was finished.

"Line up," said Miss Brown, when the bell rang for playtime. "That's right. Now – right turn – march out! Come in as soon as the bell rings – and no dawdling, please!"

"Miss Brown, have we to put our coats on, as it's a bit cold?" asked Philip. "You see, Miss Brown, I'm only just over a cold and my mother..."

"Put on your coat, cap, scarf, gloves, and boots if you want to, Philip, but DON'T FUSS!" said Miss Brown.

"Oh, but Miss Brown, I didn't come in boots," said Philip. "Do you think I ought to have? Nobody else did."

The other children marched out and soon ran into the garden to play. Only Philip was left.

"Philip, I'm so tired of you that I simply wouldn't care if you went out to play in your bare feet," said Miss Brown. "I don't even care whether you go out to play at all. In another second I shall probably tell you to sit in the corner over there and think for fifteen minutes about fussing and how silly it is."

"Oh, Miss Brown, don't do that," said Philip in alarm, and he tried to go out of the schoolroom in such a hurry that he fell over a little table and knocked down the pile of papers there.

My goodness me! How he fussed over that! "Oh dear, oh dear! Those are the papers I arranged for the painting lesson. Look, Miss Brown, they're all upset, and I did pile them together so neatly. This one's got dirty. Shall I get another sheet out of the cupboard?"

"Philip, you can stay and fuss all by yourself," said Miss Brown. "I'm going into the garden. Goodbye."

She walked out. Philip fussed over the sheets of papers and arranged them all beautifully again. Then he went to the cupboard to get a sheet instead of the one that had got dirty. He couldn't find one that was exactly the same size as the others.

"Oh dear, now that means somebody

will have a different sheet," he thought, and he looked all over the shelf to find what he wanted.

Well, by the time the bell rang for the children to come in from their play, Philip had just finished arranging the painting papers again. How upset he was when he found that he had missed the whole of playtime! He went to Miss Brown.

"Miss Brown! It's not fair! I've not had any playtime at all. I'm awfully unlucky this morning, really I am."

"Well, you're going to be lucky now," said Miss Brown, in despair. "I can't put up with you any more today. Go into the playground and play there by yourself.

You fuss so much that you don't get a single thing done – so you might as well go out and be by yourself. At least the rest of the class will be able to get something done! I don't wonder the others call you Fussy Philip! Go along out, Fussy Philip – and don't come back till you feel better!"

Philip was very hurt and upset at being called Fussy Philip. He began to cry, but Miss Brown wasn't going to have that. She took him firmly by the shoulders and put him out of the schoolroom. She shut the door.

Everybody was pleased. It was so disturbing to have someone fussing round the whole time. Philip stood outside the door, crying. He wondered what to do. He didn't dare to go back into the room again. Miss Brown really was in a temper.

He went to the cloakroom and put on his coat and cap. Then he went out into the school garden. He wandered up to the very end of it, where it was rather wild and overgrown. He sat down on a

barrow there and cried tears all down his face. He felt terribly sorry for himself.

"Hello!" said a voice, in surprise. "What's the matter? Don't cry! I can't bear to see people cry!"

Philip looked up in surprise. He saw a tiny little old woman, not even as tall as himself. She had the green eyes of the Little Folk, so Philip knew at once she belonged to the fairies. He dried his eyes.

"Old Woman, I'm very unhappy. My teacher is angry with me and she's turned me out of the schoolroom. I'm missing storytime, which is the nicest time of all the week. Now I'm here all by myself, sitting on this barrow, very lonely and sad."

"Poor lamb!" said the little old woman, and she took his hand in hers. "Come with me. I'll give you a few treats! I'm just on my way to catch the bus to go to the Silver Pixie's party. You come too! You'd love that."

"Oooh!" said Philip, his eyes shining and his heart jumping for joy. "That would be marvellous. I'll come with you now."

"Well, we've got to hurry," said the old woman. "The bus is due at the old oak-tree in about two minutes. Come along."

Off they went, through a small gap in the hedge. Philip felt very pleased. "Ha! Miss Brown has been horrid to me – but I'm going to have a good time. Won't she be surprised when I go back and tell her!"

Philip and the little old woman hurried across the field to the old oak-tree. But on the way Philip got a tiny little stone in his shoe. It really wasn't much bigger than a grain of sand, but

you know what a fusser Philip was! "Oh! I've got a stone in my shoe!" he said, and he began to limp as if he had a stone as big as an egg there! The old woman stopped at once.

"Dear dear! Let's get it out!" she said. "But, oh – I wonder if we'd better not stop. We may miss the bus."

"It does hurt me dreadfully," fussed Philip, limping badly. "Oh, dear me, what an unlucky boy I am!"

"I can't bear to see you limping like that," said the old woman. "Sit down on the bank and I'll get the stone out for you."

Philip simply loved being fussed. So down he sat and let the old woman take off his shoe. She shook out the tiny little stone, and was just going to put his shoe on again when there came a rumbling noise.

"It's the bus!" cried the old woman. "Quick, run!"

Philip jumped up and ran – with only one shoe on! He trod on a thorn and yelled! He trod on a big stone and yelled

again. "Come on, come on!" said the old woman, and pulled him across the field to the bus.

But, alas, they missed it! The bus conductor – who, most surprisingly, was a large brown rabbit – didn't see them, and the bus rumbled away without them.

"Oh, bother!" said the old woman. "It's gone. What a pity you fussed about that tiny stone! It really couldn't have hurt you. Now we'll have to walk to the Silver Pixie's, and we shall be late."

"How can I walk with only one shoe

on?" said Philip, crossly. "Have you got my left shoe?"

"No," said the old woman. "Didn't you bring it with you, you silly boy?"

"No," said Philip. "We'd better go back for it." So back they went to look for it, but they couldn't find it anywhere. "Well, you'll have to walk in one shoe if you want to go to the party," said the old woman. "Come on."

"I do wish I hadn't missed the treat of going in that funny bus," said Philip, limping along. "It had a rabbit for a conductor."

"The driver is a weasel," said the old woman. "The tickets are biscuits. You eat them instead of throwing them away."

"Gracious!" said Philip. "What a very good idea! I wish they'd do that on our buses!"

They walked on for a good way, and at last came to an enormous tree.

"The Silver Pixie lives at the top," said the old woman. "It's too tiring to climb up. We'll fly."

She undid her shawl and shook out two beautiful wings, that had been folded neatly underneath rather like two fans. Philip stared at them in surprise.

"Oooh! What gorgeous wings!" he said. "I haven't got any. I can't fly up the tree."

"I'll get you some," said the old woman, and she rapped on the trunk of the tree. A little door flew open and an old brownie peered out. "What do you want?" he asked.

"Will you lend this boy a pair of wings, Longbeard?" asked the old woman. "We want to fly up the tree."

"Come in," said the brownie, and the two went into his round tree-house. Philip couldn't help feeling excited. The brownie put a box on his table and opened it. It was full of wings of all kinds.

"I should think these would fit you," said the brownie, and he took out a pair of bright red ones. He began to fasten them on Philip's shoulders.

"They do feel funny," said Philip, beginning to fuss as usual. "They feel sort of tight."

"Well, you surely don't want them to be loose, do you?" asked the brownie. "It's not much good flying with loose wings, I can tell you! Well – try these."

He took out a pair of green ones. But Philip didn't like them very much. "I don't like green," he said. "It's unlucky."

"Green is not unlucky!" said the brownie, crossly. "Who told you that silly tale? Are the trees unlucky? Are the bushes unlucky? Is the grass unlucky?

No – they are all beautiful and happy. What a fussy boy you are! Look – here is a dear little pair of blue wings with silver edges."

They were very pretty wings, but rather small. "I don't believe they would carry me up high," said Philip. "I'd be afraid of falling down if I wore those wings."

The brownie lost his temper. He slammed down the lid of his box and threw it into a corner. "Oh, there's no

pleasing you!" he said. "I'm not lending any of my beautiful wings to a fusspot like you!"

"I'm not a fusspot!" said Philip, who didn't like that name at all. But he wasn't allowed to say a word more, because the brownie pushed him out of the tree and shut his door with a bang. The old woman looked at Philip sadly.

"You'll have to climb the tree now, instead of flying up," she said. "I'm beginning to think you're rather silly. Well – I'm off into the air. I'll see you at the top of the tree."

She flew up like an enormous butterfly. Philip began to climb the tree, wishing and wishing that he had taken the first pair of wings he had been offered.

It took him a long time to climb to the top. When he got there he was tired out. He sat down to rest on a big branch. He heard the sounds of laughter and chattering nearby, and saw that just above him on a broad, flat cloud that rested on the topmost branches, the party was going on. As he looked up, the old woman peeped over and saw him.

"Come along," she said. "I hope you're not too tired."

Philip climbed up to the cloud. "I'm dreadfully tired!" he said. "My poor arms! How they ache with trying to pull myself up higher and higher. And my left foot is sore because I haven't its shoe."

"Well, never mind, we won't let you dance or play around," said the old woman.

"Oh, but I'd like to," said Philip, looking joyfully at all the Little Folk having a merry time on the flat, soft cloud.

"No, no," said the old woman. "It would be bad for you. Look – here is the Silver Pixie. Say how-do-you-do to him!"

The Silver Pixie was a tall and beautiful creature dressed in shining silver. He even had silver hair and teeth, and he was the grandest person that Philip had ever seen.

"You must have something to eat," he said. "Hi, servants! Bring jellies here!"

Two small elves brought a big dish on

which trembled a large yellow jelly. It looked marvellous.

"I like pink jelly the best, really," said Philip, taking the spoon and plate offered him by the Silver Pixie. "But this looks lovely."

"Fancy fussing about whether the jelly is yellow or pink!" whispered an elf. The Silver Pixie turned and spoke to them. "Take this yellow jelly away and see if you can find a pink one."

The elves carried away the big dish. They didn't come back for a long time. When they arrived again, they were empty-handed. "The pink jelly is all eaten," they said to the pixie.

"Oh, well, never mind, I'll have the yellow jelly," said Philip, who by now was wishing that he hadn't said anything about the colour. But alas! When the yellow jelly-dish was found, it was empty! The guests had eaten it all!

"I'm afraid you won't be able to have any jelly," said the Silver Pixie. "I'm really very sorry. I'll have some ices sent to you."

But before the ices could arrive a tall brownie got up and clapped his hands. "Speeches!" he said. "Be quiet, everyone, while I make a speech to thank the Silver Pixie for his marvellous party!"

Poor Philip! Everyone sat still, even the servants, so no one brought him any ices or any other food, either. He was very sad. He saw the old woman near by and thought he would ask her to get him a biscuit. So he crept over the cloud to where she sat listening to the brownie's speech. But suddenly Philip reached a thin place in the cloud – and he fell through it!

Down he went, and down and down! He fell through the tree branches, *bump – bump – bump*! What a dreadfully tall tree! And then *bump*! He was on the ground. The door in the trunk flew open and the old brownie looked out at him.

"Gracious! I wondered whatever it was coming down the tree like that!" he said. "Is that the way you usually come down trees?"

"No," sobbed Philip, feeling his bumps and bruises. "Oh, what an unlucky fellow I am! I've missed every single treat I might have had! I didn't ride in that funny bus. I didn't get a pair of wings from you. I didn't get any jelly to eat at the party. And now I've fallen down the tree from top to bottom."

"If you take my advice – which you won't – I could cure you of your bad luck!" said the brownie. "I know what's the matter with you, my lad – it's fussing. Didn't you know that people who fuss always miss the best things in life? Ah, you'll miss all the treats while you're a boy – and when you grow up into a fusser nothing will ever go right for you. You're a fussy, fussy, fusser!"

Philip tried to slap the old brownie but he ran into his house and shut the door. The boy limped back to school, crying. All the children had gone home and the school was shut. Philip sat down on the step and thought hard.

"It was all because of my stupid fussing that things went wrong," he said to himself. "But how can I stop? Oh, I wish I could!"

Well, I expect he will try, but it's very hard to stop once you've really begun. So, for goodness sake, don't you be a fussy Philip, will you? I wouldn't like you to miss all the good things going – you're much too nice!

The Very
Funny Tail

"Bother! Here come those two bad children again!" said Tailer, the black cat. "Run away, everyone!"

But Paddy-Paws was asleep on the wall, his long grey tail hanging down, and he didn't hear what Tailer said. The two children came nearer and saw him.

"Look!" said Katie, "there's a fine tail to pull! Quick, pull it!"

Derek crept up to the sleeping cat. He caught hold of the hanging tail and pulled it hard.

"Wow!" yelled the cat, and leaped off the wall at once, angry and frightened.

"That's three tails we've pulled today," said Katie. "Look out for the next!"

That's what these two bad children loved to do – pull tails. They even pulled

111

cows' tails in the field, and they would have pulled dogs' tails too, if they had dared to.

All the cats were getting very tired indeed of Katie and Derek. Things got worse instead of better, for the two children really became very good indeed at tugging all the tails they saw.

Now one day a new cat came to live nearby. He was a Manx cat, and he had just a stump of a tail – for Manx cats,

as you know, never wear long tails.

The other cats came and looked at him. "You are very lucky," said Tailer.

"Why?" asked Mankie, in surprise.

"Because you've no long tail for Katie and Derek to pull," said Tailer, and he told Mankie all about the two tiresome children.

Then Paddy-Paws had a marvellous idea. "I say!" he cried. "Couldn't we play a trick on Katie and Derek? They don't know Mankie, the cat without a tail, yet. Well, can't we get a tail from somewhere and tie it loosely on Mankie, and let him sit here on the wall with it hanging down? Then, when the two children come along and pull it, it will come off and give them such a shock they will never, never pull our tails again!"

"That's really a very bright idea," said Paddy-Paws, and Sooty, Fluff and Tabby nodded their furry heads.

"The thing is – what about a tail?" wondered Paddy-Paws. "Where could we get that from?"

"I know!" cried Fluff, who belonged to

the children's own mother, "I know! My mistress has an old fur with a tail to it. I could bite off that tail and we could tie it to Mankie!"

"Good idea!" said Tailer. "Go and get the tail."

Fluff raced off. She made her way to her mistress's bedroom, and found the fur hanging in a cupboard. With her sharp teeth she nibbled and gnawed at that fur until the tail dropped off on to the floor beside Fluff.

Fluff gave a giggle. The tail looked funny all by itself. It was long and thick and silvery black. She picked it up in her mouth, and without anyone seeing her she ran down the stairs with it and out into the garden.

"Oh, good!" said the waiting cats. "What a fine tail! Now we'll tie it on to Mankie." But they couldn't seem to tie it very well because their claws kept getting in the way, so they asked the little grey squirrel to help. He was used to using his paws and he tied the tail on quite easily.

"Now sit on the wall, Mankie, and hang the tail down," cried Tailer in delight. So Mankie sat on the wall and hung the new tail down. Really, he looked rather odd, for he was a small cat, and the tail was very big and thick. Still, it looked exactly as if it belonged to him, so that was all right.

Well, soon the two children came that way home from their walk. They at once saw Mankie on the wall and they nudged one another. "Look! There's a beautiful tail to pull!" said Katie. "Whose turn is it to pull one?"

"Mine," said Derek, and he crept towards Mankie, who carefully looked the other way.

Derek put out his hand. He got hold of the tail. He gave it an enormous pull – and oh, my goodness gracious me, it came right off in his hand!

"Oh!" cried Derek, really frightened. "Katie! Katie! I've pulled the tail right off!"

Katie looked at the cat. Sure enough it now only had a little stump of a tail. She gave a squeal of fright and began to cry.

"It's got no tail now! You've pulled it off! Oh, you wicked boy!"

"Well, you'd have pulled it off if it had been your turn," said Derek, half crying too.

"No, I shouldn't. I wouldn't have pulled so hard!" cried Katie. "Oh, the

116

poor cat! What will its people say when it goes home without a tail?"

The two tiresome children were really very much upset and afraid. It was one thing to pull a tail for a joke, but quite another to pull one right off. They were so frightened that they ran to their mother, sobbing.

"What's the matter?" asked Mother at once.

"Mummy, we've pulled a cat's tail right off!" sobbed Katie.

"What? Right off?" said Mother, alarmed. "You bad, bad children! How many times have I told you not to pull tails? Now you will get into serious trouble with the cat's owner."

The children sobbed and cried, and their mother sent them to fetch the cat's tail from the lane outside, where they had left it. They picked it up and brought it to her.

"This is a strange tail for a cat to have," said Mother, in surprise. "It is more like a fox-tail – a silver fox's, I should think."

"No, Mummy, it grew on the cat that sat on the wall," said Katie. "It did really."

"Well, I'll show you how like a fox-tail it is," said Mother. "Come upstairs and I'll show you my silver-fox fur, which used to belong to Granny, and you will see how alike the two tails are."

So they all went upstairs, and Mother took the fur from the cupboard. But suddenly she saw that the tail was missing!

"The tail is gone!" she cried. "This is the tail! You cut the tail off Granny's fur, you naughty, bad children!"

"Mummy, we didn't!" cried Derek. "It came off the cat."

"I don't believe you," said Mother. "I am quite, quite sure that this tail belongs to Granny's fur. I think you have made up this story of the cat because you knew you would get into trouble if you owned up that you had taken the fur's tail."

And do you know, nothing that Katie or Derek said would make their mother believe that they had not taken the tail. She sent them both to bed early. When Fluff heard this she flew out to tell all the other cats.

"You can't imagine how well the trick worked!" she cried. "It was simply marvellous! I don't think those children will ever pull our tails again."

Fluff was right – and dear me, when poor Katie and Derek catch sight of Mankie, the cat without a tail, they feel quite ill and look the other way. Nobody has told them yet that Mankie never had a tail, so they still think they pulled it off! Didn't they get a shock?

Joanna's Nice
Big Coconut

Johnny was ill in bed, and the little girl next door was sorry for him. "What's the matter with Johnny, Mummy?" she said. "Can he come to the fair with me this afternoon? You said you'd take us both."

"No, he can't, Joanna dear," said her mother. "He has something wrong with his tummy, and he must stay in bed for a week or two till it's better."

So Joanna and her mother had to go to the fair without Johnny. Joanna went for a ride on the roundabout, but it wasn't much fun by herself. She went for a swing on the swing-boats with another girl whom she didn't know – but the girl made the swing go too high and Joanna didn't like it.

"I'm not enjoying myself very much,"

she said to her mother. "I wish Johnny was here. Oh look – what are all those coconuts for, sitting up in little cups over there?"

"That's a coconut shy," said her mother. "You get three wooden balls for twenty pence, and then you throw them at the coconuts – and if you knock one down, you have it for yourself."

"What – to take home?" said Joanna. "And eat?"

"Yes, to take home – but you won't want to eat much of it," said her mother. "A coconut is so big! Look, here is twenty pence, Joanna. See if you can knock down a coconut!"

Joanna was pleased. She gave her twenty pence to the man at the coconut shy, and he gave her three round wooden balls. She threw the first one – and dear me, it didn't go anywhere near a coconut! Then she threw her second one, much more carefully, but that didn't hit a coconut either.

"I'm no good at this!" said Joanna, and flung her last wooden ball as hard as

she could at a big fat coconut at the back. *Bumpity-bump*! It knocked against the big nut and bumped it right off its wooden cup. "Ooooh! Can I have it?" said Joanna, pleased. The man gave it to her and she ran to her mother.

"Mummy! I knocked off a coconut, the biggest of them all!" she said proudly. "And do you know what I'm going to do with it? I'm going to give it to Johnny because he's ill and couldn't come to the fair!"

"Well, he won't be allowed to eat it, dear," said her mother. "So I'm afraid it will be wasted."

"He might be allowed just a very tiny bit," said Joanna, and hugged the big coconut under her arm till she had to go home. She went in to see Johnny straight away.

"Johnny!" she said, as soon as she was in his bedroom. "Look what I won at the fair – the very biggest coconut of all, and it's for you!"

"Ooooh – I do like coconut," said Johnny. "I'll ask Mummy to break it and

we'll eat some. Oh, here she is! Mummy,
look what Joanna's brought – a coconut
that she won at the fair. It's for me! Will
you break it, please, and give me a piece.
I do like coconut!"

"Oh, darling, no," said his mother.
"You can't possibly eat coconut with such
a bad tummy. It would make you feel
very ill indeed."

"It wouldn't," said Johnny. "It would

make me feel better. I can't waste it, Mummy. Please let me have a piece. Daddy doesn't like coconut, nor do you, nor does Granny. Nobody does but me!"

"I know somebody who likes it very much," said his mother, smiling. "It won't be wasted. I know quite a number of little guests who would be glad to come and have some here."

"Who?" asked Johnny and Joanna.

"You'll see," said Johnny's mother, and she went out of the room with the coconut. Soon she was back, and Johnny saw that she had split it into two halves. Inside the rough shell was the snowy-white nut. Johnny longed to have a piece.

"No, dear, you can't," said his mother. "But Joanna can have some if she likes."

"Not if Johnny can't, thank you, Mrs Haines," said Joanna. "What are you going to do with it now? Who likes it?"

"You wait and see!" said Johnny's mother, and she went to the window and opened it. Johnny saw that she had a nail in her hand, and a hammer, and a piece of string. He and Joanna watched

carefully as she hammered the nail into the wood at the top of the window, then tied one half of the coconut with the string and hung it on the nail. The other half hung just below it.

"Now you and Joanna watch the coconut while you are playing cards," she said. "And you're sure to see a little visitor – perhaps two or three!"

Well, Johnny's mother was right! In about ten minutes there was a sudden flutter of wings, and down to the nut flew a beautiful little bird dressed in blue

127

and yellow, and with a bright blue cap. "Pim-im-im-im-im-im!" he said, and cocked a bright little eye at the children, who were watching in delight. He began to peck vigorously at the coconut. Then there came another call, and a second bird flew down – a bigger one, with more green on him, and a black cap. "Pe-ter, Pe-ter, Pe-ter-Pete!" he called loudly.

Just then Johnny's mother came into

the room and saw both birds. "Why, your visitors are here already!" she said. "Look, the tiny one is a blue tit – and the big one is a great tit. They both love coconut. You are sure to have them here every day and they will bring their families too!"

She was right. The tits were on the coconut all day long and Johnny was never dull for a single minute! He felt much better, and his appetite came back so that he ate quite big meals again.

The doctor was very pleased. "And what's made you feel well so quickly, I wonder?" he said. "There hasn't been much sunshine for you!"

"It's coconut that has put me right," said Johnny solemnly, and that made the doctor look at his mother in horror.

"Surely he hasn't been eating coconut!" he said.

"No – but my friends have!" said Johnny, and he pointed to the half-coconuts, with two blue tits pecking away and a great tit nearby. How the doctor laughed!

"Well, well!" he said. "It's a pity all ill children can't use a coconut in that way. We really ought to tell them!"

So that's why I've told you! You'll know what to ask for when you're ill – a nice big coconut hanging from a nail in your window frame!

Oh,
Mr Winkle!

Mr Winkle was always getting into trouble with Mrs Winkle – and really, I don't wonder at it! If ever there was a silly, forgetful, careless man, it was Mr Winkle! You won't believe it, but one night he put the dog into his bed, and curled himself up in the basket by the fire.

Another day his wife sent him to post some letters, and to buy some new-laid eggs. Well – he got the eggs, and when he passed the pillar-box, he posted those instead of the letters. The postman was dreadfully annoyed.

Now Mr Winkle was always losing his fountain-pen. It was most extraordinary how that pen seemed to go.

"I just popped it down on the table,"

Mr Winkle would say to his wife "– and now it's gone!"

"You mean you thought it was the poker and you stood it up by the fireplace!" Mrs Winkle would say crossly – and sure enough, there would be the fountain-pen, standing up straight by the fireplace – and the poker would somehow be on the table.

"Dear me, yes, now I remember," said Mr Winkle. "I wanted to poke the fire, and I did. Then I must have put the pen back by mistake, and popped the poker on the table. Dear me!"

"Well, it's a marvel you didn't put the poker into your waistcoat pocket!" said Mrs Winkle, impatiently. "Really, you need a nanny to look after you, Winkle."

Now this fountain-pen was always making Mrs Winkle cross because it was so often lost and so often turned up in the most surprising places. When it suddenly appeared in a rice pudding, Mrs Winkle lost her temper.

"Now, Winkle," she said, sternly, "look at that! How did your pen get in the pudding? I suppose you thought it was a grain of rice or something. Well, this is the last time you lose that pen. The very next time you want a pen and can't find yours, I shall go out and find a nanny for you. That would be a disgrace! Fancy a grown man like you having a nanny! For shame!"

Mr Winkle was dreadfully alarmed. He

couldn't bear the thought of having a nanny. No, no, that would never do. He must really be more careful and try not to forget so much. As for his pen, he must always keep it somewhere safe, where it could never get into rice puddings or by the fireplace.

He went away and thought hard about it. Then he rubbed his hands gleefully. He would buy a little chain and put it on the pen and chain the other end to his waistcoat buttonhole. Then, no matter what he did with the pen, it would always have to be with him on the chain!

"If I put it down anywhere and forget it, and walk away, the pen will have to come along," he thought happily. "The chain will pull it off the table, or off the chair, and I shall never lose it again. Oh, how happy I am!"

So out he went and bought a little chain. When he got home he told his wife all about his splendid idea, and she nodded her head, pleased.

"Where is the little chain?" she asked. "Show me!"

Mr Winkle put his hand into his pocket to get out the parcel with the chain in – and it wasn't there!

"Dear me!" he said going red. "Where's that parcel now?"

"Perhaps you've posted it, as you did the eggs," said Mrs Winkle.

"No, I didn't," said Winkle. "Oh, bless me – of course! I remember now! Look, dear, the shopman put the chain through my waistcoat buttonhole so that I shouldn't lose it. There! What do you think of that?"

Mrs Winkle was pleased. She looked at the little chain and smiled.

"Now put your fountain-pen on the end," she said, "and you'll be all right."

Mr Winkle felt for his fountain-pen. He usually kept it in his trousers pocket – but it wasn't there.

"Dear me," he said, looking worried again, "now where did I put my pen?"

"Winkle! You don't mean to say you've lost it again already!" cried Mrs Winkle. "Well, really, I shall get that nanny for you – yes, really!"

Winkle looked ready to burst into tears. He hunted round the kitchen. No pen was to be seen. He hunted in the bedroom. No pen there. He stood and thought of all the things he had done that morning. He had gone out with the dog. He had gone to the coal-cellar. He had chopped up some wood. He had read his newspaper. He had wound up the clock. He put his hands into his pockets again just to see if by any chance he had missed his pen, or there might be a hole in one of the pockets.

He felt something unusual there. He pulled it out – it was the key of the clock!

"Oh, Winkle!" said his wife, in despair. "How many times have I told you that you must put back the key of the clock when you wind it up."

Winkle ran to the clock and opened the door at the back. Placed neatly inside the clock was his fountain-pen, just where the key should be. Quickly Winkle took it out and put the key back. Then he fixed the pen tightly to the little chain and put it safely into his waistcoat pocket with a happy sigh. He had got it safely at last – and now it could never, never go away from him.

All that day and the next Mr Winkle was very happy. He didn't forget anything at all. He was as good as gold. You see, he really was trying.

On the Thursday his wife put on her hat in the morning and said she was going out to lunch with her cousin, Dame Hoho.

"I've left a nice cold lunch ready for you, Winkle," she said. "All you've got to do is to get it out of the larder and eat it. Now don't do what you did last time – give the dog your lunch and eat his plate of biscuits. Just think what you are doing. Oh, and by the way, will you write a note to your brother William, and tell him to be sure and come to tea on Sunday, because I shall be making a big chocolate cake on Saturday and I know how much he likes a slice."

"Certainly, my dear, certainly," said Mr Winkle, pleased to hear about the chocolate cake. "I'll do that as soon as you are gone."

"Well, make a note of it before you forget," said Mrs Winkle. "Goodbye!" And off she went.

Winkle thought it was a good idea just to make a note of what his wife had asked him to do – so he took out his pen and scribbled down on a piece of paper: *Write to William to tell him to come to tea.*

He put the piece of paper on the kitchen table and then sat down to read the newspaper.

It was a hot morning – and before Mr Winkle had read more than six lines his eyes closed. Soon there was the sound

of loud snoring in the little kitchen – Mr
Winkle was fast asleep!

When he woke up it was twelve o'clock.
Mr Winkle was surprised.

"Dear me!" he said. "There were such
a lot of things I wanted to do! Now I
shan't have time to do them. Well – I'll go
and get my lunch."

He went to the larder and got out a
lovely little pie, a salad and a piece of
gooseberry tart. He ate the tart first by
mistake, and then, thinking he had
finished his lunch, he went to wash up all
the dishes. He was annoyed to find he
had put his nice little pie into the
washing-up water.

"Now, Winkle," he said to himself
solemnly, "this won't do. You know that
you said you would turn over a new leaf
and not do foolish things again. Pull
yourself together!"

He went to the kitchen table and
looked at the note he had written there to
remind himself of the little job of writing
that Mrs Winkle had asked him to do.

"Aha!" said Mr Winkle. "I'll write that

140

note straightaway, so I will!" He put his hand into his trousers pocket to get out his pen – but it wasn't there.

"Dear me," said Mr Winkle. "It isn't there. Now, have I lost it again? I thought I put it in a safe place, so that I should always know where it was. But bless me if I haven't forgotten the safe place! Now was it in the soup tureen? No – it's not there. Was it in the flowerpot? No, not there either. Was it in the coal-scuttle? No, somehow I don't think I'd put it there. Now where, where, where did I put that pen of mine?"

He stood and thought, but it was no

use. He could not remember where he had put his pen.

"I must write that note to William," he said to himself. "But I can't if I don't get my pen. And whatever will Mrs Winkle say if she comes home, and finds I haven't written to William because I have lost my pen once more? She will certainly go out and find me a nanny, as she said she would – and then I should have to go to bed at six o'clock – oh dear – and wear a bib, I shouldn't wonder!"

He hunted about a little longer and then gave it up. "I shall get an ordinary pen and a bottle of ink," said Winkle. "Then I shall write the note with that – and Mrs Winkle will not know I have lost my pen – and perhaps I shall find it very soon."

But Winkle couldn't find a pen or a bottle of ink anywhere. So he put on his hat and went to ask his next-door neighbour, Dame Spink, if she would lend him them.

Dame Spink was shelling peas. She shook her head when Winkle told her

what he wanted. "I may have a pen
somewhere," she said. "I'll go and hunt.
But I know I've no ink. Will you shell
these peas for me while I go and look?"

So Winkle sat down and shelled all the
peas while Dame Spink hunted for the
pen. She came back with one, but the
nib was crossed. "Here you are," she
said. "But you'll have to borrow some
ink and another nib."

"Thank you," said Winkle, and off he
went up the hill to Mr Middle. Middle
was bathing his dog, and he wiped his
hands when he heard what Winkle
wanted, and nodded his head.

"I think I can let you have a nib," he

said. "But you might go on bathing my dog while I look. I don't want the water to get cold."

So Winkle rolled up his sleeves and began to bath the dog, who didn't like it at all. The dog tried to leap out of the bath, and poor Winkle suddenly found himself covered with white lathery soap. Then the dog shook himself violently, and Mr Winkle had a shower-bath of hot water drops! What a mess he was in!

Presently Middle came back with a nib. Winkle thanked him and tried to dry himself. Then he went down the hill to Mother Hoppy's. He felt sure she would have some ink. She was making cakes and was not at all pleased to know that Winkle wanted some ink.

"Just watch and see my cakes don't burn in the oven," she said, and went into the bedroom where she kept her ink. Winkle opened the oven door to look at the cakes – but the door was dreadfully hot and burned his fingers. He gave a yell and danced round the kitchen in pain.

Mother Hoppy came running in with the ink, and when she saw Winkle dancing about and yelling, she dropped the ink in fright, and it spilled all over her clean kitchen floor. Then she saw her open oven door and ran to shut it. Alas! Her cakes were all spoilt! She was very angry and gave Mr Winkle such a slap that he fell in the ink. He rushed out of the house, and didn't stop till he came to his friend's house. Tickles was sitting out in the garden, reading, and he jumped with fright when he saw Winkle rushing in at the gate, howling, covered with ink, soaked with water and holding his right hand as if he were badly hurt.

"What's the matter, what's the matter?" he asked. Winkle told him, and Tickles was very sorry.

"I'll lend you a bottle of ink and I'll take you home," he said. "You look very tired and upset."

He fetched a bottle of ink and then put his hand through Winkle's arm and guided him home. Winkle was very grateful.

He got out his notepaper and envelopes and set them on the kitchen table. He put the bottle of ink nearby, and laid down the pen, into which he had fitted the new nib. He meant to write the letter to his brother William at once, before he did anything foolish again.

"What's that little chain-thing you are wearing on your waistcoat?" Tickles asked suddenly, in interest.

"Oh," said Winkle, proudly, "that's my newest idea, Tickles – so clever, you know! Look, I've got a little chain, and it's fastened to my buttonhole. On the other end is my fountain-pen, so that I can't possibly lose it. Isn't that clever?"

"Awfully clever," said Tickles. "But Winkle, if you have your fountain-pen, why do you trouble to go out and borrow a pen from Dame Spink, a nib from Mr Middle, and get burned and slapped by Mother Hoppy, and run all the way to me to borrow some ink? Isn't your fountain-pen working?"

"Yes, it is," said Winkle. He sat and stared at Tickles, and then he stared at his chained-up fountain-pen. Then he stared at the pen and ink he had taken so much trouble to borrow.

"Oh dear!" he said, in a small voice. "Oh dear! What shall I do with myself, Tickles? I've chained up my pen to me so that I can't lose it – and I even forget I've got it on the chain! And I've shelled all Dame Spink's peas – and bathed Mr Middle's horrid dog – and burned myself looking after Mother Hoppy's cakes, and got covered in ink – in order to borrow a pen and ink when all the time my own fountain-pen is in my waistcoat pocket! Whatever will Mrs Winkle say?"

"Don't tell her," said Tickles, comfortingly. "I won't say a word! Now write that note, Winkle, and don't upset yourself any more."

So Winkle wrote the note and Tickles posted it. Nobody said a word to Mrs Winkle – but you should have seen her face when she saw Winkle's wet suit and ink-spotted coat!

"WHAT HAVE YOU BEEN DOING?" she said – and poor Winkle didn't know what to say!

Pull, Mr Stamp-About,
Pull!

One day little Mr Plump went shopping with his big shopping basket. He shouldn't have taken that basket because the bottom of it was falling to pieces, as Mrs Plump had often told him.

But he forgot, and took it along to the shops. He bought a nice currant cake at the baker's. He bought a bunch of carrots at the greengrocer's. He bought a box of chocolates at the sweet-shop.

Then he went to the butcher and got the Sunday joint. He didn't notice that the bottom was falling out of his basket. *Bump*! The cake fell out. *Thud*! Down went the carrots! *Bump*! That was the nice little box of chocolates.

The joint was too big to fall out. Mr Plump didn't notice his goods dropping on to the path. He saw the joint in the basket and thought that the other things were underneath.

But somebody else noticed the things falling out. That was Mr Stamp-About, who happened to be walking just behind Mr Plump when the cake dropped out. He guessed what was happening at once. Aha! There was a hole in Mr Plump's basket!

Now most people would at once have run after Mr Plump and told him what was happening. But not Mr Stamp-About. Oh no. He just picked up the cake and popped it into his own basket. Then

he waited for the next thing to drop. Hurrah! Carrots! They went into his basket, too. And the box of chocolates followed them.

Little Mrs Trot saw what Mr Stamp-About was doing, and she was upset. She was afraid of Mr Stamp-About because he had a very bad temper, but she thought she really must tell poor Mr Plump.

So she hurried up to him and whispered, "Mr Plump, you are dropping things out of your basket, and Mr Stamp-About has picked them up and put them into his!"

Mr Plump stopped and looked into his basket. Good gracious! There was only the joint there. He glared at Mr Stamp-About. "Have you picked up my goods?" he said.

"Certainly not," said Mr Stamp-About, most untruthfully.

Mr Plump looked into Mr Stamp-About's basket, and there he saw all his missing goods. He pointed at them. "You are a thief, Mr Stamp-About. Give me

them back at once, or I will fight you!"

"Pooh! I am stronger than you," said Mr Stamp-About, scornfully.

"You're not!"

"I am! You're big and fat, but you're not strong like me," said Mr Stamp-About.

Then an idea came into Mr Plump's head. "Let's prove who is the stronger of us two. I've got a rope here, see? I'll go round this corner, and you can stay here, and pull hard. If you can pull me round the corner, you can keep my goods. If you can't, I'll have them back!"

"Right!" said Mr Stamp-About, who was quite certain he could pull Mr Plump round the corner at once. He took one end of the rope and Mr Plump took the other and disappeared round the corner.

A crowd began to gather. "I'll tell you when to pull," said Jinky, Mr Plump's friend. He peeped round the corner at Mr Plump and grinned. He felt certain that Mr Plump was up to something!

So he was. He was busy tying his end of the rope to a lamp-post. Ha! Pull, Mr Stamp-About, pull all you like!

"Now – one, two, three, PULL!" yelled Jinky. And Mr Stamp-About pulled. My, how he pulled! He breathed hard, and he pulled till he went purple in the face.

Everyone yelled to him: "Pull, Mr Stamp-About, pull! Pull hard! Go on, Mr Stamp-About, PULL, PULL, PULL!"

And Mr Stamp-About pulled till his arms nearly came out. But although the lamp-post moved a little bit, it wouldn't move any more – and as for Mr Plump, he wasn't there at all!

No – he had run all the way round the next corner, and the next, and lo and behold, there he was round the third corner, just behind Mr Stamp-About, who was pulling for all he was worth. Behind him was his basket, full of Mr Plump's dropped goods. Mr Plump saw it, snatched it up, and ran off home with it, his basket of meat in the other hand. The crowd saw him and laughed, for little Mrs Trot had told them all about it.

"Pull, Mr Stamp-About, pull!" yelled everyone. "You're not as strong as you thought you were. Pull! Pull! Pull!"

Mr Stamp-About was angry. How dare Mr Plump pull against him so hard? He gave a jerk at the rope and the lamp-post moved a little. Mr Stamp-About gave another jerk, and dear me, the lamp-post shook and shivered.

"He's coming!" said Mr Stamp-About, pleased. "Aha, Mr Plump is coming! He'll soon be round the corner at a run – and then I'll pull his nose for him!"

He gave a simply enormous tug at the rope and the lamp-post came out of the ground with a crash. Mr Plod the policeman, who happened to be walking just on the opposite side of the road, was very startled to see the lamp-post jump out of the ground and then crash down.

"What's all this?" he said to himself. Then he saw that a rope was tied to it. "My goodness me – somebody is actually pulling lamp-posts up!"

He went round the corner at a run, and Mr Stamp-About, who had expected to see Mr Plump coming, was most astonished to see the policeman instead.

"Ah, Mr Stamp-About, so it's you, is

it, pulling lamp-posts up!" roared Mr
Plod, angrily. "How dare you? Are you
mad? Tying ropes to lamp-posts and
yanking them up like that! You come
along with me!"

"I didn't tie ropes round a lamp-post!"
said Mr Stamp-About, indignantly. "I tell
you I didn't."

"Well, I don't care who did the rope-
tying. It's you that is doing the pulling,"
said Mr Plod.

"But – but – I wasn't pulling at a lamp-post, I was pulling at Mr Plump," said Mr Stamp-About.

"Story-teller! I saw Mr Plump going into his cottage a few minutes ago with his shopping," said Mr Plod. "Do you want me to tie you up with that rope, Mr Stamp-About? If you don't come along with me, I will!"

"B-b-b-but," began Mr Stamp-About again, more puzzled than ever. Mr Plod didn't want to listen to any more.

"Stop your butting, or I'll think you're a goat," he said. "Come along! You'll have to pay for that lamp-post to be mended and put back again."

"Where's my basket?" said Mr Stamp-About, looking round. "Where's my basket?"

Nobody said a word. But everyone grinned and Jinky let out a great big "Haw-haw-haw". Mr Stamp-About lost his temper. He stamped and he raged, till Mr Plod took hold of his coat collar and marched him quickly off to the police station.

As for Mr Plump, he didn't go near Mr Stamp-About for a long time – and how he laughed when Jinky told him that Mr Stamp-About had had to pay for the lamp-post. It really served old Stamp-About right, didn't it?

Dame Lucky's Umbrella

Dame Lucky had a nice red umbrella that she liked very much. It had a strange handle. It was in the shape of a bird's head, and very nice to hold.

Dame Lucky had had it for her last birthday. Her brother had given it to her. "Now don't you go lending this to anyone," he said. "You're such a kindly, generous soul that you'll lend anything to anyone. But this is such a nice umbrella that I shall be very sad if you lose it."

"I won't lose it," said Dame Lucky. "I shall be very, very careful with it. It's the nicest one I've ever had."

She used it two or three times in the rain, and was very pleased with it because it opened out big and wide, and kept every spot of rain from her clothes.

Then the summer came and there was no rain to bother about for weeks. Dame Lucky put her umbrella safely away in her wardrobe.

One morning in September, her friend, Mother Lucy, came to see her. "Well, well, this is a surprise," said Dame Lucky. "You've been so ill that I never thought you'd be allowed to come all this way to see me!"

"Oh, I'm much better," said Mother Lucy. "I mustn't stay long though, because I've got to get on to my sister's for lunch. She's expecting me in half an hour."

But when Mother Lucy got up to go, she looked at the sky in dismay. "Oh,

goodness – it's just going to pour with rain. Here are the first drops. I haven't brought an umbrella with me and I shall get soaked."

"Dear me, you mustn't get wet after being so ill," said Dame Lucky at once. "You wait a moment. I'll get my new umbrella. But don't you lose it, Lucy, because it's the only one I've got and it's very precious."

"Thank you. You're a kind soul," said Mother Lucy. Dame Lucky fetched the red umbrella and put it up for her. Then off went Mother Lucy to her sister's quite dry in the pouring rain.

She had a nice lunch at her sister's – and, would you believe it, when she left she quite forgot to take Dame Lucky's umbrella with her, because it had stopped raining and the sun was shining!

So there it stood in the umbrella-stand, while Mother Hannah waved goodbye to her sister Lucy.

In a little while it began to pour with rain again. Old Mr Kindly had come to call on Mother Hannah without an

umbrella and he asked her to lend him one when he was ready to go home.

"You can take any of the umbrellas in the stand," said Mother Hannah. "There are plenty there."

So what did Mr Kindly do but choose the red umbrella with the bird-handle, the one that belonged to Dame Lucky! Off he went with it, thinking what a fine umbrella it was and how well it kept the rain off.

When he got home, his little granddaughter was there, waiting for him.

"Oh, Grandad. Can you lend me an umbrella?" she cried. "I've come out without my mackintosh and Mummy will be cross if I go home wet."

"Yes, certainly," said Mr Kindly. "Take this one. I borrowed it from Mother Hannah. You can take it back to her tomorrow."

Off went little Corinne, the huge umbrella almost hiding her. Her mother

was out when she got in, so she stood the umbrella in the hall-stand and went upstairs to take off her things.

Her brother ran down the stairs as she was about to go up. "Hello, Corinne! Is it raining? Blow, I'll have to take an umbrella then!"

And, of course, he took Dame Lucky's, putting it up as soon as he got out of doors. Off he went, whistling in the rain, to his friend's house.

He put the umbrella into the hall-stand and went to find Jacko, his friend. Soon they were fitting together railway lines, and when Pip said goodbye to Jacko, he quite forgot about the umbrella, because the sun was now shining again.

So there it stayed in Jacko's house all that night. His Great-aunt Priscilla saw it there the next morning and was surprised, because she hadn't seen it before. Nobody knew who owned it. What a peculiar thing!

Now, two days later, Dame Lucky put on her things to go out shopping and visiting. She looked up at the sky as she stepped out of her front door. "Dear me – it looks like rain!" she said. "I must take my umbrella."

But it wasn't in the hall-stand. And it wasn't in the wardrobe in her bedroom, either. How strange! Where could it be?

"I must have lent it to somebody," said Dame Lucky. "I've forgotten who, though. Oh dear, I do hope I haven't lost it for good!"

She set out to do her shopping. It didn't rain while she was at the market. "Perhaps it won't rain at all," thought Dame Lucky. "I'll go in and see my old friend Priscilla on my way back."

She met Jacko on the way. "Is your Great-aunt Priscilla at home?" she asked him.

"Oh, yes," said Jacko. "She was only saying today that she wished she could see you. You go in and see her, Dame Lucky. You might just get there before the rain comes!"

She went on to the house where her friend Priscilla lived. She just got there before the rain fell. Dame Priscilla was very pleased to see her. Soon they were sitting talking over cups of cocoa.

"Well, I must go," said Dame Lucky at last. "Oh dear – look at the rain! And I haven't got an umbrella!"

"What! Have you lost yours?" asked Dame Priscilla. "How unlucky! Well, I'll lend you one."

She took Dame Lucky to the hall-stand, and Dame Lucky looked at the two or three umbrellas standing there. She gave a cry.

"Why! Where did this one come from?

It's mine, I do declare! Look at the bird-handle! Priscilla, however did it come to be here?"

"Nobody knows," said Dame Priscilla in astonishment. "Is it really yours? Then how did it get here? It has been here for the last two days."

"Waiting for me then, I expect," said Dame Lucky, happily. "Isn't that a bit of luck, Priscilla? I shan't need to borrow one from you. I'll just take my own umbrella! Goodbye."

Off she went under her great red umbrella, very pleased to have it again. And whom should she meet on her way home but her brother, the very one who had given her the umbrella!

"Hello, hello!" he cried. "I see you've still got your umbrella! I should have been cross if you'd lost it. Let me share it with you!"

So they walked home together under the big red umbrella – and to this day, Dame Lucky doesn't know how it came to be standing in Dame Priscilla's hall-stand, waiting for her!

Knots
in his Beard

Sleepy the brownie had a very long beard. It reached almost to his feet, and sometimes when he forgot to go and have it cut it nearly tripped him up.

Sleepy forgot a lot of things. His memory was a very, very bad one. Next door to him lived Slick the goblin. He had a wonderful memory and never forgot anything.

Sleepy didn't like Slick because he laughed at him. The goblin would come and poke his nose in at the door and say, "Hello! Is your house on fire, or have you just forgotten you're baking a cake, Sleepy?"

Then Sleepy would see that his kitchen was full of smoke, and he would rush to the oven and take out the burnt cake.

"Ha, ha! You're a funny one, you are!" Slick would say. "That's the third cake you've forgotten about this week."

"How do you remember things, Slick?" Sleepy asked the goblin one day. "I don't believe you forget anything, do you?"

"I remember everything," said Slick, but that wasn't true. For one thing, he didn't remember to pay his bills, and he often forgot to feed his dog and cat.

"Tell me how to remember things," said Sleepy. "Is there a trick about it?"

"Well, some people tie a knot in their hanky, and that reminds them to do something they want to do," said Slick. "For instance – I wanted to remember to go and call on Dame HoHo today, so look – here is a knot in my hanky. That's to remind me, you see."

"That's very, very clever," said Sleepy. "But I hardly ever use my hanky. I never have a cold, I never sneeze, I never cough. I might put twenty knots in my hanky and I'd never notice them!"

"Well, my dear Sleepy, put a knot in ur long beard, then," said Slick, laughing. "You'll notice that, won't you? Then, when you see the knot, or feel it, you'll say, 'Ha! That was to remind me to order some wood – or to get some cocoa.' And off you'll go to do it. You won't forget anything if you put knots into your beard."

Well, Sleepy thought he would try it. Yes, it seemed a splendid idea. He would put a knot in his beard the very next time he wanted to be sure to remember something.

Well, that afternoon he remembered that he ought to go and see his Aunt Old-One sometime the next day. So he carefully put a big knot in his beard.

Aha! Now he would remember all right. But when the next day came he had quite forgotten what the knot was for. He felt the knot with his fingers, frowned and muttered – but no, he could not remember why he had put it there. He called to Slick over the fence.

"Hey, Slick! I've got a knot in my beard, and I don't remember why. Do you?"

Slick grinned to himself. He looked at the knot very hard and nodded his head. "Yes, yes, Sleepy – you put that knot there to remind yourself that you were going to give me three new-laid eggs. Don't you remember?"

"Good gracious! Did I really?" said Sleepy. "No, I don't remember that at all. Dear, dear, what a forgettery I have! I'll get the eggs at once."

Slick laughed loudly when he took the eggs indoors. This was going to be funny. He hoped that Sleepy would put some more knots in his beard. He took the trouble to look over the fence next morning to see if he had.

Yes, there was another knot in his beard. He called to Sleepy. "Hey! Do you remember what that knot is for in your beard? Think hard now."

"Oh dear! Is there another knot in my beard?" said Sleepy, anxiously. "Now what can it be for? More bread from the baker. No, he's been. Sausages – no, they're in the larder. Did I put it there to remind me to water my flowers? No, it has been raining. What is it there for?"

"I know," said Slick. "You put it there to remind you to let me have three fresh lettuces out of your garden. Fancy

forgetting that, Sleepy. I didn't like to remind you."

"Did I really say that?" said Sleepy, thinking that he must have felt very generously towards Slick. "Oh, well – you'd better get them."

Slick went into the garden and took six lettuces. Sleepy wasn't looking, so he didn't know. Mean old Slick!

"I'm not going to put knots in my beard any more," said Sleepy, as Slick walked by his door. Slick was sorry about that. He had just begun to make a nice lot of plans about knots in Sleepy's beard!

That afternoon Sleepy brought out a deckchair and put it in the sunshine. He sat down and fell fast asleep. His long beard waved in the wind. Slick saw him there and grinned.

In a flash he was creeping into Sleepy's garden and tiptoeing up to the snoring brownie. In a twink he had put two knots in his beard just near the end. Ha! They would puzzle Sleepy when he woke up.

They did. They puzzled him so much

that he didn't eat any tea for worrying about them. Two knots! Were they for two things, or for one very big thing? He simply couldn't remember.

Slick looked in at the kitchen door. "Hello, Sleepy! Have you forgotten that you said you'd pay me for the weeding I did for you the other week?"

"What weeding?" said Sleepy. "You

never did any! I don't remember saying I'd pay you, either."

"Well, look, there are the two knots you put into your beard – one to remind you to pay me, and the other to remind you what it was for," said Slick, grinning. "Pay up, Sleepy, and don't pretend you've forgotten."

"I'm not pretending! I have forgotten!" said poor Sleepy, getting up to fetch his purse. "I've even forgotten how much I owe you."

"Two pounds," said Slick, and Sleepy

groaned. Oh dear, oh dear – two pounds for weeding he had forgotten all about! He paid them to Slick and then took the knots out of his beard.

Slick waited till he saw Sleepy fast asleep again next day and once more tied some knots in his beard. This time he put four in, and when Sleepy woke up he felt them in horror. He looked down at them, wondering what in the world he had put them there for.

Slick looked over the wall. "Hello! You haven't forgotten that you asked me in to tea, I hope? Ah, I see you have a knot in your beard to remind you. What are the other knots for, Sleepy?"

"Do you mean to say I asked you in to tea?" said Sleepy, amazed. "Whatever came over me? I must have been mad! I haven't any cakes in the house, anyway."

"Well, I expect that was what the second knot was for – to remind you to buy some cakes," said Slick at once. "And the third one was to remind you to make egg sandwiches."

"Hm! And what was the fourth one

for?" said Sleepy, crossly. "I suppose you know that too?"

"Oh, yes!" said Slick. "It was to remind you to ask me to clean out your hen-house for you."

"I don't believe it!" said Sleepy.

"Well, how would I know what the knots were for if you hadn't told me?" said Slick.

"Ah well – I suppose you couldn't know if I didn't tell you," said Sleepy, puzzled. "Anyway, go and buy some cakes and I'll make the egg sandwiches. But I've changed my mind about the hen-house. I'm going to do it myself."

"Right," said Slick, pleased to find that he was going to have a very good tea. "I'll go and get the cakes."

Off he went, and while he was gone Sleepy's Aunt Old-One came along. She sat down in his kitchen.

"I believe you've forgotten that you asked me to tea, Sleepy," she said.

Sleepy groaned. He did remember asking his aunt to tea – but there didn't seem to be a knot in his beard for that!

"Sleepy, why have you knotted your beard like that?" said Aunt Old-One, looking at it in surprise.

Sleepy told her about the knots. He also told her that he didn't remember putting them in, he didn't remember what they were for, and that he had been told all sorts of things by Slick.

"Aha! I know that fellow Slick!" said Aunt Old-One. "A bad, bad young goblin he used to be, and he's no better now than he ever was. He's playing tricks on you, Sleepy, but you're too silly to know it. I'll tell you how to pay him back!"

So she told him – and how he chuckled! He was still chuckling when Slick came in with the cakes. He wasn't at all pleased to see Aunt Old-One. He was afraid of her.

They began their tea. Presently Slick noticed six enormous knots in Sleepy's beard that hadn't been there before. He was surprised.

"What's that knot for, Sleepy?" he said, pointing to the first one.

"That's to remind me of somebody who owes me quite a bit of money," said Sleepy, grinning.

"And what's the second one for?" asked Slick.

"That one is to remind me of somebody who borrowed my ladder, and this next one is to remind me of someone who borrowed my kettle," said Sleepy.

Slick didn't like this. He had borrowed the ladder and the kettle! He decided not to ask about the other knots. But Aunt Old-One soon told him about them.

"The fourth knot is to remind him that he ought to shake somebody till his teeth rattle, and the fifth one is to tell him to be sure and chase him round the room with a stick."

"And the sixth one is to remind me of the name of this person," said Sleepy, suddenly getting up. "Let me think now – yes, it's Slick! Ha – where is that money you owe me – where are my ladder and my kettle? Where is my stick to chase you with? Aha!"

Slick fled out of the room, Aunt Old-One was ready with her stick as he passed by, and she gave him such a poke with it that he leaped in the air and yelled.

Sleepy fell into his chair and laughed till he fell out of it.

"Slick won't bother about knots any more," said Aunt Old-One. "He'll never mention them again. And I guess he will bring back the ladder, the kettle and the money before I go. He'll be afraid of my stick if he doesn't."

The ladder, the kettle and the money were all outside the door before Aunt Old-One went. Sleepy was very pleased. He kissed his aunt and thanked her.

"Now don't forget you are coming to see me tomorrow," said Aunt Old-One. "Tie a nice little knot in your beard – but don't ask Slick what it's for!"

Do you suppose Sleepy will remember what it's for? I'm sure he won't!

The
Little Toy-Maker

George and Fanny were excited because their mother had said they might go out for a picnic by themselves. "If you cross over the road very carefully and go to the hill above the Long Field, you should be all right," she said.

So they set off, with George carrying the picnic basket. In the basket were some egg sandwiches, two rosy apples, a small bar of chocolate, and two pieces of ginger cake. There was a bottle of lemonade as well, and George and Fanny kept thinking of the cool lemonade as they crossed the road, went through the Long Field and up the hill. They did feel so very thirsty.

There were ash and sycamore trees up on the hill. Already they were throwing down their seeds on the wind – ash spinners that spun in the breeze, and sycamore keys that twirled down to the ground. George picked some up and looked at them.

"Aren't they nice?" he said. "Throw some up into the air, Fanny, and see them spin to the ground. The tree is pleased to see them twirling in the wind, because then it knows that its seeds are travelling far away to grow into big new trees."

After a while the children sat down to have their lunch. They began with the egg sandwiches, but before they had taken more than a few bites they saw a most surprising sight. A very small man, not much taller than George's teddy-bear at home, came walking out from behind a gorse bush. He carried two baskets with him. One was empty and one was full. The full one had sandwiches and milk in it, and the children thought that the small man must be having a picnic, as they were.

The little man didn't see them. He had a very long white beard that he had tied neatly round his waist to keep out of the way of his feet. He wore enormous glasses on his big nose, and he had funny pointed ears and a hat that had tiny bells on. The bells tinkled as he walked. Fanny wished and wished that she had a hat like that.

"What a very little man!" said Fanny. "Do you suppose he is a pixie or a brownie?"

"Shh!" said George. "Don't talk. Let's watch."

So they watched. The little man walked along humming a song – and suddenly he tripped over a root and down he went! His full basket tipped up, and out fell his sandwiches and milk. The bottle broke. The sandwiches split open and fell into bits on the grass.

"Oh! What a pity!" cried George, and ran to help at once. The little man was surprised to see him. George picked him up, brushed the grass off his clothes, and looked sadly at the milk and sandwiches.

"Your picnic is no use," he said. "Come and share ours. Do!"

The small man smiled and his face lit up at once. He picked up his baskets and went to where the children had spread their picnic food. Soon he was sitting down chatting to them, sharing their sandwiches, cake, and chocolate. He was very pleased.

"Why was one of your baskets empty?"
asked Fanny. "What were you going to
put into it?"

"Ash and sycamore keys," said the
small man. "There are plenty on this
hill."

"Shall we help you to fill your basket?"
said George. "We've eaten everything
now and Fanny and I would like to help
you."

"Oh, do," said the small man. So the

three of them picked up the ash and sycamore keys, and put them neatly into the basket.

"Why do you collect these?" asked Fanny. "I would so like to know. Do you burn them, or something?"

"Oh no. I'm a toy-maker and I use them for keys for my clockwork toys," said the little man. "Come along home with me, if you like. I'll show you what I do."

He took them over the top of the hill and there, under a mossy curtain, was a tiny green door set in the side of the hill. The little man pushed a sycamore key into the door and unlocked it. Inside was a tiny room, set with small furniture and a big work-table.

And on the table were all kinds of toys! They were made out of hazelnut shells, acorns, chestnuts, pine cones, and all sorts of things! The small man had cleverly made bodies and heads and legs and wings, and there were the toys, very small, but very quaint and beautiful. The children stared at them in delight.

"Now, you see," said the little man, emptying out his basket of keys on to his work-table, "now, you see, all I need to do is to find keys to fit these toys, and then they can be wound up and they will walk and run and dance. Just fit a few keys into the holes and see if you can wind up any of the toys."

In great excitement the two children fitted ash and sycamore keys into the toys, and George found one that fitted a pine-cone bird perfectly. He wound it up – and the bird danced and hopped, pecked and even flapped its funny wings. It was lovely to watch.

Soon all the funny little toys were dancing about on the table, and the children clapped their hands in joy. It was the funniest sight they had ever seen! They only had to fit a key to any of the toys, wind it up – and lo and behold, that toy came to life!

"I wish we hadn't got to go, but we must. Mum will be worried if we're late," said George at last. "Goodbye, little fellow. I do love your toys."

"Choose one each," said the little man generously. So they did. Fanny chose the bird and George chose a hedgehog made very cleverly out of a prickly chestnut-case and a piece of beech-mast. It ran just like a real hedgehog when George wound it up.

And now those two little toys are on their mantelpiece at home, and they are so funny to watch when George and Fanny wind them up with ash or sycamore keys. I can't show you the toys – but you can go and find ash and sycamore keys for yourself if you like. There are plenty under the trees, spinning in the wind. Find a few, and see what good little keys they make for winding up fairy toys!